T0354311

Clean

Clean

A Novel

Laura Otis

CLEAN
A NOVEL

Author Photo by Joe Boris © 2012 www.JoeBoris.com

iUniverse books may be ordered through booksellers or by contacting:

iUniverse
1663 Liberty Drive
Bloomington, IN 47403
www.iuniverse.com
1-800-Authors (1-800-288-4677)

ISBN: 978-1-5320-6383-1 (sc)
ISBN: 978-1-5320-6384-8 (e)

Library of Congress Control Number: 2018914461

Print information available on the last page.

iUniverse rev. date: 01/08/2019

For hotel and motel housekeepers everywhere

1

I push open the door to find the bathroom sink glowing like a blue altar. Someone has left the light on again, and its wave of bleach spills onto the bed, which has been kicked up into white foam. You can learn a lot about a person from the way she leaves a bed. Some women make it themselves and pull the sheets so tight they seem ashamed of their sleep. I always know they've been in there, though, from the tiny little hairs they leave. I know from the grit that sticks to their skin and drops away in the night. They take pride in leaving the room pristine—but no one sleeps here without a trace.

This bed looks more like the ones where people want to get their money's worth. $45.99, $39.99 on the net, says Jake. And for that, they tear up the bed like some gangster hid his treasure there and they have thirty seconds to find it. I brace the door with my cart and gather the liberated sheets. The dry gray blanket scratches my hands, but the sheets are cool and smooth, glad to be remembered and washed. *Last night we took a beating,* they say as they fall limp into my hands. They've been marred by two sex stains, round spots that spread under girls and dry into sad, pale suns. In the folds cling long and short black hairs that couldn't have come from one head. One lies strung out like a snake, but another is bunched into a crazy ball, as though trying to hide from the scissors. A kinky one looks like it just fell from a rusty Brillo pad. Clinging to the blanket are a curled brown leaf and the wispy carcass of a spider. One of these people has slept on the floor, maybe down in back under the hangers. The wind blows in all sorts of loose, dry things, and they always gather in that corner. If two women and a man slept here, one would end up down there with the dead bugs, unwanted.

I have to hurry, since Luz says no more than half an hour per room. Sixteen a day, half an hour each, just get through your goddamn quarter. "What are you doing there, scrubbing the walls? My kids can clean faster than you!" Her boys probably clean just like she does, rubbing like she's scratching an itch. Luz doesn't understand what these rooms need, the kinds of damage people do.

I rake back the scrunchy shower curtain and raise the lever on the tap. Water swishes, and I wet my yellow rag, the best hair catcher I've got. That's my main job in the tub—capturing each defiant hair. Whoever built this shower had sense: smooth, creamy walls, no grubby joints. Against its gleaming sides, dark curly hairs stand out like ants that invaded some kid's milk. A kinky brown hair lurks in the corner, tense as a rattlesnake coiled to strike. I spritz the walls with pink germ-killer spray whose strawberry smell masks its force. Long, firm swipes with your fingers spread—that's the way to wipe a wall. Brillo has been here, plus both black-haired girls. Unlike his, their hair hasn't stuck, but I pull it from the drain in a soapy string. That's it for the hairs, and the shower thanks me, wet and gleaming white. With its pale brown polka-dot curtain, it reminds me of a coffee drink with whipped cream.

Now for the toilet, whose smooth white skin is crusted with Brillo's mustard pee. I spray its lips with strawberry, and it winces. Funny how much a toilet looks like a face. White, round and upright, eyeless maybe, but with a wet mouth waiting to be filled. *Zzt. Zzt.* I spritz it with sour green and massage its insulted cheeks. I mistrust the strawberry to dissolve the splats of this idiot who missed the bowl. Blue pad now, my special toilet pad, too filthy for a shower or wall. Along the white rim, like a shrinking string of beads, coil red-brown drops of blood. Not from a period, stringy purple black. Those must have oozed from a cut.

Ten minutes. The mirror disappears behind circles of choking white foam. My glove and forearm open silver streaks, where my flushed face appears in flashes. I turn on the water, and the sink monster growls and sucks the stream in a swirl. I wipe the counter's pale brown surface and grimace as its digs catch the sponge. No new ones, just that same old triangle of gouges made by the corners of something hard. A hammer? A vise? Guys clean their tools here, and the sink has to choke down the muck. No spots on the counter, no toothpaste blobs. Someone has swabbed it clean. Almost everyone leaves something here, mascara tracks or black razor dust. Why wipe a counter if they know I'm coming? Did someone try to write her name in blood?

Five minutes. The vacuum roars to scare the dirt out of the rug. Whatever's hiding down there is going to cling to the fibers and fight. The vacuum catches orange tortilla chip crumbs and inch-long thread worms from people's clothes. But it misses the coffee, makeup, and blood that turn a rug to a hard, angry thing. With a yellow cloth I rub down the drawers, where crumbs and grit can hide. I pick up the lamp, a hefty jug whose jagged base would shred my rag. To get the dust out of those pottery grooves, I'd need a whirling brush like Manny uses down at the car wash.

As long as people can't see the dirt, they're happy. There can't be any visible trace. $39.99 buys them the feeling that the room is completely theirs. No one has ever slept in it before, and no one will ever sleep there again. They put up with TVs that pull pictures like taffy and music that pounds through the walls. But one springy hair in the shower, and they're calling Jake at the front desk.

Jake oversees the Run-Rite Inn about every hour he can. He arrives for checkout, sometimes before six in the morning, and stays until check-in is well advanced. As the day manager, he knows every hinge on each door and the personality of each room. Our night managers roll through like semis, never forming a connection with the place. They study at the community college in Jones City, tense young guys who can live without much sleep. Probably some drug helps them bond with the computer all night and drive fifty miles each way to do it. When Jake appears in the morning, they must feel as good as grass warmed by the sun. Corporate may own the Run-Rite Inn, but it's Jake's motel.

Jake smiles knowingly when he tells me about people's complaints. The blacker and kinkier the hairs they find, the more likely they'll say the room's not clean. He has yet to hear anyone gripe about a sleek blonde hair that might have dropped from Marilyn Monroe's head. Jake's smile spreads to a grin. "But not in your rooms." He meets my eyes, and we stand connected, the only ones who know how to treat this place. In the five years I've been working here, no one has ever complained about my rooms.

I run to grab fresh towels from my cart. I'll have to steal five minutes from 222. Ten minutes, if I'm going to dump this blanket. My shoulder sets the hangers jangling. I seize the trash buckets, and their liners whisper. They're too light, so I set them down. Nothing is in them, no tissues, no soap wrappers, even though the waxy soaps have been used. I run my fingers over the rustling liners, but I can feel no stickiness. Underneath each bag, one of the spares is gone. I've seen people take out their trash before, but never replace the bags.

I pace my way back through the healed room, soothing the air with vanilla spray. Two bath towels, two hand towels, two washcloths, crisp and white. I run my palm over the restored counter, cool and smooth. The bed draws a breath, and the fluorescent light blinks. They tell me they're ready for another day. They can stand one more night of kicking and gouging.

"I'll be back tomorrow," I whisper to the lamp, which sits sullen under its dusty hat.

2

Luz stands on the walkway with her arms folded, her hips pressing the concrete wall. Texas wind has freed wisps of black hair, which flutter around her troubled face. Bright-pink nails burrow into her brown skin. At ten o'clock, the fresh swish of traffic washes off most of her Spanish. Only the brightest tones penetrate, hot needles in the morning air.

"¿En la ba-*su*-ra?" she yelps at Marielena.

Mari isn't wearing her Run-Rite Inn T-shirt. A black-and-blue dress covers her small, curved shape. The dark skirt sculpts her round behind, and little hills swell the pale blue top where sequins flash. Her long black hair flies free in the wind, hiding her wet, red eyes.

"¡Sí!"

Mari's light voice arcs toward the sky, and I wish I could understand her frightened patter. Jake says if he could go on attitude alone, he'd ask corporate to make me head housekeeper. But for now Luz has to be in charge because she's got the communication skills. Probably she doesn't even see that cube of tomato her gold sandal is squashing. The guy in 218 must have dropped it, the one with the taco bag in his trash. After a day of roofing and hours on the road, he was probably so hungry he gulped his food on his way up the stairs. Luz never notices things like that, but she can yell at Marielena.

"¡No me mientas!"

Seeing me adds to her frustration. She puffs out her lower lip and blows a hot stream.

"What's going on?" I ask.

Luz scrunches up her mouth. "She says she found that dress in the trash. Somebody threw it out. She wants to keep it."

"¡Sí!"

Desperate for an ally, Marielena focuses her red eyes on me. The jeweled blue against her soft brown skin makes me draw in my breath. My palms tingle. How perfectly those sparkly mounds would fill the cups of my hands. Whoever designed that dress must have had Marielena in mind. To peel it off her would be a crime. But we could get in trouble. Nobody threw that dress out.

"Really? You found it in the trash?" I squint.

"¡Sí! ¡Te lo juro!" she cries.

Compared to Luz's, Marielena's fine tones barely penetrate the traffic's rush.

"We have to tell Jake," I sigh. "Whoever left that dress will want it back. We should leave it at the front desk."

Luz's dark eyes snap. "We have to tell Jake." She throws my words back in a Spanish shape. "Why do you always have to tell him everything? You hot for him or something, *chata*?"

My face burns, and my throat closes. Luz barks at Mari, who ducks back into 225. That must be where she found the dress, gleaming in a heap on the floor. I would have done the same thing at eighteen, just stopped working and pulled it on. I breathe deep and wait for a semi to scour past, blowing out puffs of black smoke.

"I just think he needs to know. Somebody might call. Are you really going to let her have it?"

Luz steps forward from the wall. "Nobody calls here about stuff they left. This isn't that kind of place."

She's right—this isn't the kind of place that people come back to or that women want to recall. Marielena emerges from the room and looks pleadingly at Luz. The head housekeeper nods.

"She can keep it. You have any idea what she's been through? Where's she going to get a dress like that?"

Luz keeps her black eyes fixed on me. My nose prickles, and my eyes swell.

"Okay." My voice dissolves in the traffic's fuzz.

"Don't you fucking tell Jake," hisses Luz.

3

I wheel my cart down to the elevator and bump it over the sill. As the doors close, I gather a breath and hold it through the tense hums and creaks. I don't release it until the gray wings part, as if I were blowing myself free. In the laundry, I hand Pili the sheet rolls, and she nods, revealing broken teeth. The searing light brightens her yellow hair, which contrasts with an inch of coffee roots. I pass her the blanket, and the black crescents of her eyebrows rise. Against my fingers, the gray thing feels as though someone sucked all the cool, wet life out of it. I point at the floor and circle my hand. Pili laughs, sending tremors through her breasts and belly. She tosses the blanket into a canvas bin, where it lies stiff and confused among the sheets.

My foot splats in a dark puddle in the breezeway. Where does all this water come from? In any weather, murky lakes form here, fed by the laundry or last week's rain. Maybe they just ooze up from the ground, drawing butts and tortilla chips to form soup. It doesn't help that Janet stands here, full of chips, peanuts, and chocolate.

Jake gave Janet her name because of a movie he knows. One day this little guy was buying his breakfast, a bald man with a bristly mustache. I was rumbling by with a loaded cart, and Jake was talking with Frank, the maintenance man. Janet can be perverse in the morning and suck up dollars but keep her spirals turned tight. The bristly man was the sort to feed in more dollars rather than complain the first time. With a whine, Janet slurped up his last bill.

"Damn it!" He thumped her silver side.

Jake straightened and glared.

"Damn it!" The man kicked her metal skirt.

"Hey!" yelled Jake.

Frank suddenly chortled. "Damn it, Janet!"

Jake doubled over with laughter. He doesn't laugh much, and it warmed me to see his belly shaking and his face so bright.

"Damn it, Janet!" He and Frank wavered around as if they were drunk. The guy at the machine lost his furious look and began to laugh with them. I've never heard Jake make so much noise, especially in the morning, when he could wake people. I must have looked shocked, because when he saw me, he laughed harder.

"It's a movie," he gasped.

He refunded the man five dollars even though he had lost only three.

In the office this morning, Frank is already spewing his ugly thoughts at Jake.

"Jesus, what a … dogs!"

My cart bangs Janet's metal edge, and I realize it's knocked a chunk from Frank's voice.

"Uh-huh …" Jake's lower tones die behind the wall.

I roll my cart back and forth until it's safely lodged behind Janet.

"I mean, fuck—the little one ain't bad, but she don't speak a word of English. And Jabba the Hutt and that dominatrix … The only one I can talk to looks like a doughboy with his face squashed in. Where do you find these women?"

I creep up to the glass door and glimpse Frank's hard blue shoulder.

"Come on, ease up," says Jake. "We hire 'em to clean. If you were a hot woman, would you work here?"

"Shit." Frank's voice slices the air, whereas Jake's folds into it like smoke. "Couldn't you find just *one* it doesn't hurt to look at? It's bummin' me out, starin' at these bitches."

"C'mon, man. What do you think you look like?"

I straighten my arms and push through the door.

"Hey, Ginny!"

Jake's round face brightens. He presses his palms against the counter, tensing the muscles in his thick arms. Unlike Frank, he swells his blue Run-Rite Inn T-shirt, since he has quite a belly for a guy his age. Under his curly brown hair, his eyes look ready to decide anything except their color. Jake's lips curve in a half smile.

"Anything else I need to know about?" he asks Frank.

"Nah. I think you got the picture."

Frank shifts sideways to pass me, although he's got plenty of room.

"How's it going, Ginny?" asks Jake.

He folds his fleshy arms. His eyes dart to the computer and then back to me, scanning me from wind-blasted hair to wet feet.

"Okay." I nod. "I … Something bad happened last night in 220."

"Oh, yeah?" Jake straightens. "What makes you think so?"

His eyes make my insides quiver.

"I … There were three …"

"Somebody had a threesome?" Jake's grin melts his tension. "Nothin' bad about that."

A gleam from a heart-shaped leaf draws my eye. Opposite the computer, a fake philodendron holds together in a waxy green cluster.

"But they … Someone slept on the floor!"

Jake laughs, his eyes bright with mischief. "Yeah, that tends to happen. Three's a lousy number."

"But how many did they pay for?" I ask.

Jake reaches for his mouse, and his mind shifts to the screen. "Two twenty?" He finds the record faster than he can frown. "Two people."

"That's not right," I mutter.

Jake clicks his way through his computer world. His mouth opens, and I smell peanuts and chocolate. He snaps his world shut and returns.

"They've checked out. I think we should forget about this one. If they were here, I could charge them extra. But once they're gone … Maybe it was a family."

"This wasn't a family."

The big, dark families never bother me, six or seven in a car. Three or four kids, sometimes a grandma. They fit as many as they can in a bed, and the rest sleep down on the rug. They leave red-and-white-striped chicken buckets or two or three spicy pizza boxes. All in all, they batter the room less than one angry drunk with a bottle.

"How'd they pay?"

Over Jake's head, the round white clock says it's 10:37.

"Cash."

He runs a strong hand through his curls, which rise up before they're squashed flat.

"Why do you care so much about these people? You find any ziplocks in there?"

"Nah. They took out their trash."

Jake freezes, his fingers rooted in his hair. "They took out their trash?" He laughs. "Shit! Well, I guess we could dumpster dive. You really that curious?"

"Place just gave me a bad feeling." I shrug.

"Well, let it go." He sighs. "Listen." He beckons me behind the counter. "You want to see something worth thinking about? Take a look at this."

I raise the hinged panel and slip behind the counter. Jake clicks, and an indigo world blooms. In it, a dark-haired boy points to an iPad, and a smooth-skinned girl strains to see. His T-shirt and her scarf harmonize with the background like glints in an ocean of blue. "Nye Means Business," reads a ribbon running across the page.

"What is this?" I ask.

"Nye University." He smiles. "You study online, at your own pace. No basket weaving, no bullshit, just stuff you need. In two years, you earn a business degree."

From I-50, a motorcycle hurls an ugly splat of sound.

"But doesn't that cost a lot of money?"

I need to get back to my rooms. I have thirteen to go before check-in, and Luz is going to be pissed.

"Yeah."

Jake pulls his eyes from the screen to look down at me, full on. Heat rises and burns my cheeks. The sunlight blasting through the front windows reveals every red-brown hair on his arms.

"I'm gonna do this," he vows. "No matter what. I've got some stuff goin' on."

The words and pictures dissolve into blue, and the letters rush into new forms: "The world is changing. Why not lead that change, in the spirit of creative enterprise? Transform the world as you transform yourself. Let your vision make an impact."

"Look at these courses." Jake's voice rises. "Innovation. Marketing. Leadership."

"Sounds great." I nod.

Jake draws a quick breath. "It's not about the courses. It's about who you are, what you want, how you use your time. You can learn a lot managing someone's hotel, watching the decisions come down. But do you want to spend the rest of your life acting out someone else's decisions?"

My "no" is breath with a hint of sound.

"This place is decent, and we try to keep it that way." He pauses for a reflective smile. "But if I'm ever going to lead my own chain, I've got to start now."

"Wow."

Jake's intense gaze pulls at me. "For three weeks, you can try their courses for free. This one on leadership is amazing. Did you know, no one can make you feel afraid? No one can make you feel anything. Anything you feel, it's up to you."

"I-I don't know about that."

I picture the unmade beds flapping at me, demanding to be smoothed.

"You could do this." Jake's voice still won't settle. "How long have you been housekeeping? If you could do anything, what—"

The phones ring in a chorus and flash at each other with worried lights. Jake glances at the caller ID, and his voice reverts to low calm as he answers.

"Yeah? Oh, fuck." His fingers grip the phone. "Yeah, okay, I'll be right up."

He cuts off the caller with his thumb and summons Frank to the front desk.

"What happened?" My throat feels dry.

"Oh, some guy's drunk up in 219. Or on drugs. Or both. Luz found him, and he won't get out."

In a corner of his screen, tiny, dark figures say 10:57. In tourist season, we'd have a rush around now, but in March everyone has left early. Makes sense—working people have to leave before seven. It's the battered ones who get caught in the sheets, the ones for whom time doesn't matter.

"Ginny," Jake says to me, low and smooth, "I'm gonna need you."

"What about Luz? Can't she go?"

"Nah. This guy's a gringo. She said he was wearin' a suit."

Jake raises the panel for me and Frank, who has slouched in from the breezeway.

"No games," Jake warns Frank. "Anyone who comes in here, you treat 'em like royalty."

"Yeah, right," smirks Frank. "Royalty with forty bucks a night in their expense accounts."

The steps clang under Jake's and my feet, and the flimsy stairway shudders. We strike the planks exactly together like two soldiers on the march. A sour whiff slips from Jake's jeans, which are just ahead of my nose. Silently we move down the external walkway and pause, one on each side of the door. Jake sighs and digs the white key card from his pocket.

"Manager! Open up!"

The gray-brown door rattles under the heavy thumps of his fist. Room 219 doesn't make a sound, so Jake shoves the card in its slot. A pale green light flashes.

"Manager! I'm comin' in!"

Jake pushes the door open as though he's clearing an obstacle. The smell of vomit has turned the air to sludge.

"Hey! What the fuck!"

A stubbly man grips the covers and glares with angry alarm. The lost ones always retreat to the bed, like survivors clinging to a raft. This one looks more desperate than most—I think his binge grabbed him by surprise. On the rug, his gray jacket and pants lie twisted, looking as though they've been kicked. He's got every light on and the TV lisping to show the force of his melted will. In the bluish light, every pore of his flushed skin looks ugly. Sweat and oil have turned his black hair to tentacles flopping around his bald spot. A square whiskey bottle flashes on the nightstand, but nothing breaks the blue field by the sink. Empty hangers bear witness, their silver elbows poised. Fiercely, he clutches the gray blanket.

"What the fuck is this?" he yells. "You can't do this!"

"Hey!" Jake steps forward, and the door slams. "You watch your language. There's a lady present."

"I want to stay another night!" The man's black eyes pulse. "You're violating my privacy!"

"You can't stay another night." Jake keeps his voice tight and low. "You have to leave right now."

The flushed face curls with disgust. "You're not going to tell me this place is full?"

The vomit smell oozes into me, bringing pictures of pale, chunky goo. Where am I going to find it this time? Half dried on the itching toilet cheeks or blown into the wall's sticky daubs?

Jake folds his arms and shifts his weight. "We're not full. But we reserve the right to refuse service. I hear you've been using abusive language with our housekeepers. We can't have that. This is a family place."

The man's red arm reaches for the bottle, and I raise my arm to protect my eyes. Instead of producing a whiplash motion, his gesture dissolves into shivers. With a clatter, he replaces the bottle on the nightstand and brings his hands to his face.

"I was clean," he sobs. "I-I was clean."

"You can get clean again, Mister," I murmur.

Jake nods to me, and I pick up the bottle, its neck warm and greasy under my fingers.

"It's checkout time," Jake says softly. "Time to go. You need a place to stay, the Roundabout will take you. But you can't stay here."

Jake takes a tentative step forward.

"Get away from me!" The greasy, red face turns savage.

"Come on, man. Don't make me call the cops. Neither one of us needs that."

The blanket drops from the man's hand, and his chest heaves.

"Come on, bro. I'll give you an extra half hour. Clean yourself up. We've got coffee downstairs. This lady here needs to clean the room. Whatever's goin' on, you can fix it."

The man shakes his head mechanically and stares at his limp hands.

"I can't believe …" he murmurs. "I can't believe …"

A gleam from the nightstand catches my eye, the elegant black curve of an iPhone. I creep around the foot of the bed. The whiskey bottle makes a glassy clunk as I set it down beside the sink. There's the vomit, a crusty beard on the toilet, plus lava on the bathtub, floor, and wall. More sludge has erupted onto the counter and is choking the helpless sink. The amber soup seems not to have been sprayed by a man but by some kind of perverse hose. A few soft-edged logs are turning in the toilet, which he has chosen not to flush. With sickening, furious insistence, the waste of his body screams, "I was here!"

I withdraw from the room ahead of Jake, who shoots a glance back at the trembling man.

"Half an hour, man. If you're not out by then, I'm callin' the cops."

The man has drawn the gray blanket back around him. I wonder what came out of that black iPhone to send him into this state.

Jake leans on the railing and gazes up at the insistent traffic on I-50. Over its gentle arch, two halves of a gray house are sailing, so perfectly split they seem to have been cut by a meat cleaver.

"Can you clean up in there?" he asks.

In crescents under his arms, his blue Run-Rite Inn T-shirt has turned a shade darker.

"It's not in my quarter. I'll have to ask Luz."

Jake smiles warmly, and I realize I'm gripping the whiskey bottle. He extends a hand.

"I'll talk to her. Marielena couldn't handle that, and Luz …" He takes the bottle and studies it, musing. "You know, that guy had an iPhone 6. What a friggin' waste."

"You think he'll get out?"

The second half of the house reaches the crest, its orange flags flapping in the wind.

"Oh, yeah. He's not a fighter."

Jake breathes out hard, and I catch another whiff of gas that the wind didn't scatter.

"Ginny, you handled yourself well in there."

In the bright sunlight, Jake's eyes are pure green. On the wall behind his legs, the gray paint looks like ruffled lichens.

"Ginny. Look at me. I'm trying to tell you about an opportunity."

I raise my eyes to his round face.

"The Haverford Inn needs someone to help with breakfast. They called me about it last week. Five to ten. You could do it before your shift here. Would you be interested in that?"

Jake certainly took his time telling me. He couldn't have been thinking about the others. Luz has her boys, and the silver-haired people at the Haverford want someone who understands when they ask for butter. It would mean starting late, then scrubbing away at the grubbiest rooms Luz can pick. Even now she tries to sniff out the filth and give the easy ones to Marielena.

Wow, the Haverford—even their parking lot looks crisp, like a baker's box around a mocha cake. But the tiredness! Black, shrinking cold at four in the morning; you alive, everyone else asleep. I've worked the early shift before, and "shift" means you're shifted to a different world. First you're pumping, racing, rushing, when everyone else is still. They start to catch up at ten o'clock, when you move on to your second job. By late afternoon, you're swimming in syrup, while they all charge ahead. At ten you grasp your pillow like it's an angel who will carry you off to sleep. But before you spin into blackness, you realize that tomorrow, it begins again.

"Can I think about it?"

"Yeah, but they'll need to know soon." Jake frowns. "Why don't you sleep on it, let them know tomorrow?"

The divided house drifts down the interstate, its fiery flags fading like receding eyes. The stairs clang in an uneven rhythm, and a messy crash sounds as the bottle lands in the dumpster. I go back to my rooms and save 219 for last. Based on Jake's description, Luz knocks two rooms off my quarter. Instead of cleaning those, I can disinfect the poor room that has turned to a pigsty overnight. As I push the vacuum cleaner back and forth, I picture the drunken man slinking out. I doubt he has the energy to do more damage, but when I open 219, he's left a warm batch of vomit in the sheets.

I strip the bed down to the mattress and carry the bundle to Pili. I can't make out her words, but I understand her hot sounds as her black eyes rake the sheets. For the bathroom, I pull on my pink rubber gloves, since the brown crust looks toxic. Once it's wet, it dissolves after four or five passes, but after each wipe, I have to free the sponge of stringy brown seaweed. Sometime last night he hit the taco place. Wisps of lettuce are turning in the drain. The spin slows, and the water settles. The poor, oval sink is choked. Considering what people try to force down its throat, it's a wonder it can keep on swallowing. With my finger, I push a shred of lettuce across the cool lake that has ceased to spin. For an hour and a half, I scour the toilet, the wall, the floor, and the tub. After each sortie, I service my fighter sponge at the gushing bathtub tap. My eyes are burning, and my nose is running, but I wipe it against my upper arm. I just want to get through this and find Frank to help the poor, choked sink.

4

Where Frontage Road meets the Merrill Highway, the hard-edged sidewalk just dies. It ends neatly, with a full square of cement waiting mutely for a neighbor. Frontage Road, which doubles back on I-50, ends up exactly the same way. Trim, dark asphalt gives way to weeds in a sudden, blunt divide. I can't tell you how many people have left the Run-Rite Inn for the interstate only to end up in loose grass. Their tires have beaten a makeshift trail that dissolves into sandy curves.

Beside the Merrill, my feet and others have smoothed a brown trail where the concrete ends. Every day I walk down this slope, where the Merrill peels off the swishing freeway. As I make my way downhill to the strip, my eyes comb the weeds scratching my feet. Dust has already coated my toes, which are grinding paste against my brown sandals. It pays to search the dry, brittle hair that the land around here seems to grow. It catches anything that will fly out a window: tissues, sticky wrappers, and stunned, battered dolls. Once I found a twenty-dollar bill doubled around a stem, neat as a flag.

A burst from a motorcycle jolts my eyes up. A black-and-silver bike curves past the Roundabout Inn, where the Merrill bends to parallel I-50—Business 50, they call it, four miles of places where you can stop instead of go. In Arrow, the interstate bubbles out to avoid blasting through what's left of downtown. On a map, the Merrill Highway looks appealing, a straight line through an old Western town. Our strip forms the taut string of a bow from exit 91 to 95. It may be straight, but with cars coming and going, it's not exactly a shortcut.

The barred balconies of the Roundabout slice the sky, and I wonder if the greasy man will land there. Without a company to rule it, the Roundabout vibrates like a queenless hive. The brown motel has never found a manager who can establish order there. The Roundabout will take anyone, even people who stink, scream, and shake. Their rooms house skinny, yellow-toothed women; angry men on disability; twitchy mothers with kids trying to hide. A woman with bleached, clumped hair draws on a cigarette and tracks me from her gray perch. I suppose the Run-Rite Inn would look this bad if the people staying there wouldn't leave. We get the workers, the construction crews, people who want to sleep and move on. In summer, we see scruffy students and tourists. One look at the Roundabout would send those smooth-breathing people zooming west to Jones City.

A frizzy-haired boy on a tricycle grinds his way across the parking lot. *Scaggity, scaggity, scaggity.* Grit collects in the Roundabout lot where the wind can't scour. Two stories, brown shingles, a gently sloped roof, external walkways with protective rails. In its shape, the Roundabout looks like the Run-Rite Inn, except that its soul is sick. The dark-skinned boy starts jerkily at a pop from a passing car. He turns his bike back toward the ground-floor rooms. *Scaggity, scaggity, scaggity.* What makes this place so shabby is the people chafing against it day and night. The building never gets to stand alone and cut clean lines against the sky. Bodies are always slouching in and out, off to Scooter's for a drink or to the taco place. Feet never stop shaking the stairs, kicking the doors, or crushing the cringing rugs. I wouldn't want that black-haired drunk on the road, but I hate to think of him here.

Guys like him turn up pretty often, but not with iPhone 6s. The pawn shop in the Dollar World Mall exerts a magnetic pull. If he isn't careful, that smoky jewel will land there, with the guitars behind the black mesh gates. It'll join the gold chains and silver computers that people sell for gas to reach Jones City. For some people, losing the most precious things they have isn't as bad as ending up here. I raise my eyes to a crest of signs against the sky: Pete's Pawn, Arrow Cards and Gifts, Taquería Norteña. A dark bird glides over the stores, toward the back streets of small, wooden houses. What's so bad about living in Arrow? I've seen worse places than this.

I pick up my pace when the sidewalk returns, thanks to the fried chicken and taco stores. I want to get the new girl at Never-Ending Nails, not that old woman whose voice gouges me like her steel spatula. The new girl appeared a few weeks ago, a beauty with quick fingers and slim arms. I sense that her touch will feel as good as her soft stillness, her serene face. But word is out up and down the strip that our nail parlor has a new technician. Once work lets out, all kinds of women will be thrusting their feet in her face for $15.99 plus tip.

Dull bells clunk against the glass door, and a sharp-edged voice calls, "Hi!" The old woman beams at me like the rows of bright bottles behind her. With her bun of black hair and round, neckless body, she stands like a queen in the world she's built. Along the green wall in back sits Donna on a black-cushioned throne. I often see this tall housekeeper on the strip, and her friendliness warms me. Hunched at her feet, the new girl turns to shoot me a shy smile. Quickly she goes back to her work, spreading color with a tiny brush. If she's already painting, she can't take much longer. The old woman reads my mind.

"Nice to see you! Judy can take care of you today. You pick color, and she be ready. She be ready by time you pick."

"Hey, Ginny, how are you?" calls Donna. "Pick a color and get back here."

No matter how many times I come here, I'm never ready for the choice. In their rack, the gleaming bottles edge forward, hoping to be pulled. Every color calls to me with its own voice—brash pink like Bugs Bunny, midnight blue like Sade. My fingers stroke the curved bottles, trying to feel the colors. "Clack!" they say as they knock together. I want warmth that isn't loud, a voice that doesn't have to rise to be heard.

"Try a whole bunch of 'em!" calls Donna. "She can do a different color on each toe!"

My fingers stop over a purplish rose. They close on the bottle, and the others sigh. My smile comes from the inside this time as I think what the next hour will bring. Sitting in Never-Ending Nails always feels like resting in a tree. Only the back wall is green, but a strip of lime around the other three holds the place together like a vine. Near the front window, philodendrons have sent out Rapunzel shoots so that their heart-shaped leaves hang in rigged

25

loops. Six hopeful black chairs with tan basins sit waiting for princesses to arrive. By the register, a fat golden cat marks time by waving his blunt paw.

The chair next to Donna cushions me from the crown of my head to my heels. I wiggle my toes in churning, warm water. How funny we must look to this girl—long and freckled, short and pale. The only thing we have in common is nails, since Donna uses her body in ways I never would.

Donna cleans at a lot of motels, but Jake won't have her at the Run-Rite Inn. "It's her extracurricular activities," he grimaces. If I looked like Donna, I wonder if I'd try it too. She's got a proud neck, long legs, and an action hero's face. If I were a guy, I'd give her everything I had. Only her noise would bother me, since Donna is louder than an early-morning jay.

"Check it out! Peppermint!" She punches my arm.

Across Donna's red toenails, the quiet girl is painting white stripes like lines of icing on a cake. A few wisps of black hair have escaped her bun and settled onto her sleeveless blue blouse. Bent over Donna's feet, she breathes softly as she forms the lines. Her slender back lies motionless as she paints each stripe, then rises as she pauses between them.

"Great!" I smile. "Special deal?"

"Yeah." Donna frowns. "I thought I was gonna have fifty bucks, but this asshole stood me up."

"Shit."

A truck clears its throat as it cruises past the hard brown edge of the Haverford.

Donna's forearm tenses against the chair. "Fuckin' internet," she mutters. "Told me that he got another date online."

"Could you try that?" I ask. "Maybe put a picture …"

Donna shakes her head. "Too many freaks. I wanna see 'em first."

She gazes down as she remembers something, and I hope that she can read them right. I could never let strangers push inside me the way that Donna does. Anyone who gets close enough to touch me, I want to beat off with a bat. Donna stretches her long arms toward her toes, which wiggle with their own life. I can see what she's saying—as long as she can choose, Donna belongs to herself.

Judy raises her head and turns from Donna to me. My throat tightens, and my eyes sting. What did she do for God to get a face like that? Broad black eyes, ceramic curves, slender golden-brown arms. She's slim but smooth all over, as though an expert hand shaped her flesh. A sky-blue butterfly clip holds her hair. Her blouse is fastened by pale blue buttons. She motions for me to raise my foot onto a white towel above the basin. With silver nippers, she snips away the loose skin on my toes.

"So what's new at your place?" Donna raises her feet to admire her candy cane nails.

"All kinds of weird shit," I mutter. "Someone threw out a black-and-blue dress. Another bunch took out their own trash."

Donna's guffaw jolts me. "No way! Wish my people would do that. Mine just throw their shit around the rooms and run off with the sheets and towels."

From a plastic bottle that looks made for ketchup, the girl squeezes a dot of orange goop onto each toe. She spreads it delicately and pushes firmly at my cuticles with a tool that looks like a spoonbill's beak. My insides curl toward the delicious, caring hurt. Orange scent spirals into my nose.

"You ever work at the Haverford?" I murmur.

"Yeah," sighs Donna. "That place was great. They don't pay you more than anywhere else, but it's just … nice. You don't feel like you're knee-deep in shit."

I don't ask her why she stopped working there, and Donna doesn't say. She pushes herself up and pads over to the dryer, where the old woman is beckoning.

I close my eyes and enjoy the gentle jabs until a pull tells me to lower my foot. Strong fingers repeat their motions on the left, and I wonder how it feels to trim five toes twice. Every pair of feet has its quirks, but tending them must be like cleaning rooms with two toilets. Sure enough, she adds a variation this time and files my left nails with tickling strokes. My laugh shakes my legs, and she looks up at me with a half smile.

"Your name is … Judy?" I ask.

She freezes in mid-stroke, and her smile vanishes. "Út," she whispers. "Judy for here." Her lips curve again as she resumes filing. She seems to be warmed by an inner laugh.

"How about …?" I jerk my head toward the old woman, who is reordering colors in the rack. With her fingers spread, she stands with the concentration of someone seeking notes on a keyboard. Judy follows my eyes, and her smile broadens.

"Hồng," she murmurs. "Heather for you."

She turns her dark eyes down and squeezes rose cream into her palm. With spread fingers, she rubs at my calves from the ankles all the way to the knees. The rose and the rubbing make my legs so happy that their hard, round swells want to cry. A strange business, being touched by a person you can't talk to. I wonder if she cares what there is to me beyond these stubby white legs and feet.

The old woman calls to her from the front desk, and she answers with a high-pitched mew. Their voices sound light and delicate, catches of breath and curdled coos. Of course, she could be saying that I have the ugliest feet she's ever seen. But I don't think so. Under her care, my clean toes look beautiful, round and pink with curved shields.

Judy reaches for the heavy silver nippers, and my lower back melts into the chair. Lips tense, she snips off every bit of skin choking the lovely moon plates. Between the silver jaws, a mound of sticky, unwanted shreds rises. The heap grows until she's cleared all ten nails. Then, with her index finger, she whisks it off.

"See ya! You be good!"

Musical clunks follow Donna's farewell. She'll be headed for Scooter's, where I hope she'll make money. The guys around here don't have much to give, and she would do better to head west. When she goes, I'm going to miss the sound of her jaunty, musical voice.

Judy covers my foot with gritty, orange gel and scours it with a gray pumice stone. She scans it for hardness and attacks each callus with a silver lollipop grater. Like soft cheese, the dead, wet skin snows into the water. I breathe more quickly as she jams a rubbery green form between my toes. With expert licks, she paints a base coat, then layer after layer of rose. The trouble is, I've never found a color as pretty as a woman's hands make me feel. Like all of them, this rose disappoints me, calling up the blue from my skin.

Judy feels my sadness, and her bottle of color clacks against the tray. In each hand, she grips one of my ankles and shakes it. Her wide black eyes meet mine, and she smiles anxiously and makes curved sounds. Don't I like the color? If I'm unhappy, Heather is going to give her hell. I smile at her and flex my toes, as much as I can in the stiff green frame.

"They're beautiful," I say and give her a frayed five-dollar bill.

Judy tucks it in her shirt pocket. I'm not sure what changes the color of her face, her blush or her sudden smile.

5

I can't take my eyes off my toes, which gleam pink in the late-day sun. In the golden light, they're jewels in a brown leather frame, and I can't believe that they're mine. This aging light is kinder than the blue-white blast of overhead strips. If only my sandals were clean enough for these glowing circles of color. After just a few steps, my feet are grinding grit and dust into paste.

The pink gems are too pretty to hide, and instead of taking me home, my feet carry me east toward Main. I pause at the light, where the Haverford Inn stands across a river of traffic. What's left of Arrow hangs below the Merrill in a loose basket of streets. A few stores have survived, and an old white house screened by porches holds a history museum. Some ladies who fight to keep the place alive have raised money for buckets of purple flowers. But the shops around the plaza don't sell things you need. Antique stores, they call themselves, full of pasty figurines and mossy smells. If you shop there, it's to seek shelter from the wind and finger knickknacks no one wants to keep.

The Catholic church watches over the plaza with pink towers that defy the dust. Its gates are closed, but seven is a funny time, the day exhausted and the sun still burning. The antique shops have gone gray and still, and a silver padlock links the gun shop's gates. Up on the Merrill, cars are seeking motels, and people at dinner are eying their last brown fries. Those who live here have settled into silver softness, waiting for the good shows to start. Only birds are out in the air, pecking pieces of bread too big to snatch.

A bunch of them are chirping in the plaza at the feet of a man in a gray suit. Without a hat, his bald head must be searing, even in this late-day light. Between his thumb and finger, he's rubbing a bun to bits for a chirruping brown horde. Kneading the ground, my pink toes cross the street and crunch down the plaza's gritty path.

Dressed and combed on the battered bench, the man from 219 looks like a different soul. Only his sorrow gives him away, his loose, hapless tears at the bun. He keeps flicking even when my shadow brushes him, although most of the sparrows have fled. His eyes rise only when he realizes that he's dropping crumbs into empty dust.

He gazes up, too tired to be startled, until his recognition catches. Images tumble and fall into place. I guess I look different in a blouse and jeans, without my Run-Rite Inn T-shirt.

"You …" he starts. He coughs to clear his voice, but once he frees it, it collapses.

"You feeling any better?" I murmur.

"Yeah. No." He shakes his head and drops the remnants of his bun into a white bag. "I … I'm sorry," he whispers.

"It happens."

Our voices are as dry as the wind in the overhead leaves. He looks toward the gazebo, which stands like a prize where the plaza's two paths meet. A fountain would be nice here, kids screaming in the spray, but this isn't that kind of town. I press my toes against the leather in waves, one after another. Overhead, the wind hisses through leaves that hang like brittle blades. The man jerks his chin toward a nearby plaque.

"That all true on there?" he asks. "The guy shot by Comanches who recovered here—his arrow's buried under that wooden birdcage?"

"No," I whisper.

Luz told me different. Jimmy Merrill got shot, but not by Comanches. He called the town Amparo after the woman he loved—until she shot him when he married a white girl.

"I didn't think so," he mutters. "Those things never are."

Three sparrows land at his feet as though blown back by a gust of wind.

"Why are you here?" I ask.

He frowns at diamonds of sky cut by the gazebo's withered wood.

"I-I just need some time to think."

He looks at me as though trying to mold a thought out of flowing water.

"You need some help, they got a group down at the Bible church—just before the interstate—near the trailer park."

I don't usually speak this many words at once, and they knock together on the way out.

"Thanks." He smiles ironically, and I can't tell whether he's insulted.

"You got a place to stay?"

This time his smile looks real, and I imagine happiness on his dark face. People who've never known joy give a different light, like a summer morning that brings rain.

"Not yet. But I've heard great things about the Roundabout."

"Don't go there!" My words rush out. "Go to the Haverford. And stay away from Scooter's."

"Okay." He nods, gripping his crumpled white bag.

He reaches into his breast pocket for his iPhone.

6

The door to my room shrieks as though I stabbed it, but once it shuts, no one knows I'm here. I slide the chains closed and flip the dead bolts, one-two-three, starting at the top and working my way down. Those clicks are my favorite sounds of the day, confirmations that my work is done. Light from the overhead bulb brightens a space just big enough for me to turn around. In the far corner, brightness catches the curve of my sink and the white shower cabin Manny installed. Manny likes having me live behind his body shop and says I'm better than a cat and dog both. I scare off the rats, but I don't say a word about the men who meet there at night.

When I first came to Arrow, I cleaned Manny's shop in the late afternoon to make some extra cash. I liked the looks of his shoulder-length brown hair and wiry arms with snake tattoos. I admire a guy who knows how to bring crushed cars back to life. All kinds of men work for Manny, since he attracts the sort who don't stay long in one place. Disheveled white guys mostly, with sunburned skin and eyes that won't lock onto things. Some of his men have arms thicker than Jake's, but I wonder how they force metal back into shape. They move in jerks like frightened kids transported into strange men's bodies.

To clean Manny's desk, I asked for some gunk that they use to rub black grease off their hands. As I squatted, wiping a steel leg, I turned and caught one of them watching me from the shop. The brown-haired kid held his wrench like a lollipop that he wished he could lick. When our eyes met, he blushed and shifted his wrench from hand to hand. He looked away, but not with disgust—more like I was his mom and he was scared that I would belt him one.

Toward dusk, men would start gathering in the shop. Work turned to a party as the day faded to dusk. Manny shooed me away at first, but with time, he trusted me to clean during the party phase. Bursts of laughter drove me as I rubbed black prints like a killer erasing his tracks. Manny's men didn't laugh deep and low like Jake—their squawking sounds made me smile. A bunch of girls might laugh like that if one described her math teacher's backside.

Manny has an ease that guides him as he restores the shapes of bashed cars. He never shudders at the gouges. Nothing can scare his eyes off.

One night, I could feel him watching me as I strained to dust his highest shelves.

"You're real quiet," he said. "Where do you go at night? What do you do when you're not here?"

"I stay at the Run-Rite Inn," I said. "They give me a room for half my check."

"Let me show you something," said Manny.

He led me around back and shouldered open a door that gave a sickening scrape. Light fell on black walls and greasy sacks draped across dead motors. A metal table and two folding chairs spoke of some strange business conducted here. A dusky mouse darted from one heap to another, and I felt a pang.

"If I hauled off this junk, got you some plumbing, would you consider living here?"

Under a jagged scar, Manny's brown eyes watched me think. No one would ever know that I lived in this room. No one could find me in this dark hole—no one would look. I could restore this poor room to life, and I could keep what I earned. The place was an oily horror, but once I scoured it, it would be mine.

Manny sensed my agreement, but he wanted to be sure. "You know what this place is?"

"A place for men . . . who like men?" I asked. My throat was almost closed.

"Yeah, that's right." Manny smiled and folded his arms so that his blue snakes swelled. "And you wouldn't tell anyone?"

I shook my head, and my brown braid flew free.

"Yeah, I didn't think so." Manny breathed roughly in and out. "And you don't like men—I mean, at least ..." Something in my eyes dissolved his voice. "I know a place, for women, if you'd like that."

"No. No," I said quickly. "I like it here."

"Well, good," said Manny. "I could rent it to you for almost nothing. It'd be better for the place, have someone around at night."

The room he showed me looked as though someone had tried to smother its soul. Without a window, it hadn't seen light in years, and only mice and bugs had touched its skin. I nodded more at the walls than at Manny, standing with his shoulder to the door. Already I was scouring in my mind, wondering what each stroke would reveal.

Manny and the brown-haired boy cleaned out the trash, exposing a forgotten sink and frantic mice. Nothing on four legs has ever frightened me, and I whispered to them as I scrubbed. Manny lent me a ladder, and with Soft Scrub, I took back the walls block by block. Bleachy foam ate through the grease, and cement appeared, looking like scared cottage cheese. The blocks seemed aghast at their nakedness, so I asked Manny for some paint. He gave me gray for the floor and white for the walls. We had to leave the door open for a week, and he drove out two drifters who tried to move in.

Manny screwed in three different locks, and he set up the toilet and shower. The furniture I found at a secondhand place: a kid's bed, a scratched wardrobe, a wooden table and chair. Manny offered me the metal table in the room, but its legs felt cold to the touch. I've always hated the chill of metal against my skin. Manny sold the table to used-furniture people, and I guess it moved on to the trailer park. With my hot plate and heater, I brought the place to life like Frankenstein electrifying his monster.

Luz keeps asking me how I can live in a garage. She and Pili live down at the trailer park with most of the Mexican people in town. Luz is always after me to share a place with some woman or other. The trailers have windows with flower boxes and red curtains that warm the light. But one good storm would send those tin cans flying. Manny's shop has cinder block walls, and it's cemented to the strip. Besides, I could only afford a trailer if I shared, and that would mean living with someone's sounds. The chatter of her TV when I came home, the swish of her shower, the sizzle of her dinner. The sighs of her breath would scratch my skin at night. At Manny's, the sounds are all mine.

My shopping bag crackles as it settles, and I pull out a package of fig bars. I set my purse on the chair and brush my hair in slow strokes that match my breaths. Unless the mice have come back, no speck in this room has stirred since I left this morning. I ease into my nightgown and switch on the first episode of *Forensic Team.* A low voice tells of stabbings, shootings, and rapes. The killers always get caught, sometimes by women who swab up DNA. The *Forensic Team* voice soothes me like the cars and trucks swishing past on I-50. After ten, the traffic on the strip dissolves, but the interstate flows all night.

I settle in bed with a stack of fig bars pressed so tight together they can hardly breathe. I bite off a corner, and sweetness fills my mouth. The voice is describing a little girl who got killed riding her bike. The driver who hit her roared away, but scientists are tracing black paint on her mangled wheel. It's cool tonight, and four blankets press me. That's the sweetest part of the night, lying surrounded on every side like the filling of a hot apple turnover. I run my palms over my thighs to assure my legs that everything's fine. My hands pause on my belly to read the scars. Those came from the Sinking In. Those bumps run over every hidden part of me like dead, sprawling white worms. I raise the blankets with my toes and wiggle them, imagining my nails' bright rose. My feet are the only part of me he never touched—on an ugly girl, the ugliest thing.

I swallow another cookie, and with my free hand I squeeze my breast. If I worked at the Haverford, I'd be too tired to think. I would swim through the days until I drowned. But what if their manager liked me? What if he asked me to leave the Run-Rite Inn? Who would I talk to without Jake? Yet Jake seemed to want me to go.

The Run-Rite Inn rooms would sicken without me, black slime on the grout, crumpled shirts under the beds. Luz won't go down on all fours to check, and Marielena is scared of what she might find. One day it might be a sticky condom, and an inspector from corporate might seize it. Then they would fire Jake, and the only thing he'd ever manage would be a broom. In this room, black sludge would creep up the walls; auto parts would settle; mice would rebuild their nests. As if I had never been here at all. Dust and mold and crumbs and grease, as if I had never been here.

7

Thud! I wake up with a gasp. Something is yanking at the door. Maybe another drifter outside is trying to escape the wind. The people living out on the highway must be so cold tonight. *Ba-dump!* The door rattles in its frame. The room is breathing, the door straining against its bolts. I flap the blankets to cool myself, then throw them all aside. Soon I'm shivering in the air that comes streaming through the cracks. Every jolt of the door spurs my heart. Sounds like someone is tearing it from its hinges.

Between bumps, I listen for traffic, which comes in whispering waves. Traffic doesn't rise in sighs like the wind. It surprises you like the exhaled breath of a shell against your ear. The traffic waves soothe me as I float in the dark, and I scan them for special sounds. Bright-eyed animals are gliding past, strong and fierce in the night. A truck sobs, and I picture its trailer, its tires scouring the road. Each passing thing speaks with its own voice. A car gives a gentle call; a semi, a sharp, tenor cry. The biggest trucks sing many notes at once, a sliding rainbow of sound. Motorcycles hack the night to bits, but no bike is thrashing the air tonight. In the next wave, only a convoy of trucks moans.

In the dark, the blue numbers read 3:12. If I worked at the Haverford, I'd be getting up soon. I see myself unlocking the kitchen, pulling on a green apron, scrubbing my hands. All those extra hours will exhaust me, but I already know I'll take the job. The door shakes, and I strain to hear the trucks' voices. I need them to guide me through the haunted hours until the light comes again.

8

In the green Haverford breakfast room, no one knows what to do with the lids. A salty smell draws people to the bins, where they raise the tops to peek. Fingers of blue flame warm silver tureens that I have filled with baby omelets and hash browns. Under the lids lie crisp potatoes and neatly folded yellow flaps. After a night of fretting in their rooms, people savor that smell as they would a hug. Men hold the silver lids like cymbals while they pause to breathe it in. To dig in, people have to lay down the lids, and they look right and left, confused. I like to watch them as they take this test. Some guys call their wives to hold the lids. Others lower the lids and walk off, muttering. Some set one lid wobbling on another until it slides off and crashes.

The women head to the colder corner, to the glass case of yogurt and bowl of fruit. Like the men, they hesitate. *Yoplait or Activia? How bitter are those grapefruit slices?* Their eyes tell me everything as they glance at their hands, their husbands, their cars outside. If they ran, it would be more from their kids than from the poor fools holding the silver cymbals. Their kids rush straight to the waffle iron, shaking the floor with their thudding steps. The hot machine calls for help all morning like a baby bird menaced by hawks.

You wouldn't think that making waffles could be so

tough. One plastic cup of batter, clap the iron shut, flip it, and wait until it peeps. But the waffles stick or lie abandoned until they begin to sear. Every square of that mold holds tight to its cake as though the waffle were its closest friend. When I pry the squares free, I feel as though I'm separating lovers.

While the mothers hunt fruit, the kids pour batter on the counter and spin the peeping iron round. They do the most damage at the cereal bins, where one turn of the handle frees a few flakes; and another, a crisp avalanche. "Mom!" wail the kids when Cheerios have filled a bowl and spilled onto the counter. What to do with the mound is another test. Some Moms tip half the bowl in the trash. A few look quickly from side to side, raise the lid, and dump the cereal back in the bin. Once, long ago, a roaring voice must have warned them never to waste food.

The star of the breakfast room is the toaster, which draws men, women, and children alike. I could watch it for hours, the creeping grill that turns pale slices to crisp brown squares. On the first trip through, so little happens that most people opt for another round. The slice turns gold, then a deeper brown. Black grill marks spread, but the toast can only creep, trapped under the blazing coils. People forget toast more than anything else, or maybe they just stop wanting it. The slice they set moving slides down, dry and hard, but no hand comes to pick it up.

Slippery lids, rushing cereal, charring toast. It's like the whole world is busting loose. Everything's jumping out of its place, and I'm the one in charge. For a week, a Haverford manager trained me before she would let me work. At the Run-Rite Inn, when Jake hires you, you go to work the next day. Here, a thin lady in a gray suit taught me how to talk to Haverford guests. "Haverford guests," she kept calling them, as though they were staying for free. No matter how dumb or mean they were, I couldn't tell them they were wrong. If anyone got crazy, I should call a manager. Otherwise, I should do what they said. I was representing the Haverford Inn, and I was the first person they would see all day.

In the corner farthest from the food, a bald man sits with his back to the wall. He holds a white mug to his lips as though he were kissing it rather than drinking. He watches a downed plane on the TV screen and rubs a green napkin with his free hand.

"Hey, you made it!" I realize I'm smiling.

The man jumps and spills coffee on the mat. He freezes as if he were a mouse and I were a swooping hawk.

"Hey, it's all right," I say.

He sets his coffee down and watches the brown wave splash the white rim. Gray stubble pierces much of his face, and his bald spot gleams with oil. He keeps his eyes on his stiff fingers, which he's spread as though testing their strength.

"Don't you want anything to eat?" I ask. "The waffles are good."

He raises his eyes, bitter black. "Do you not have a life or something? Is that why you're following me?"

I tense but remember he's a Haverford guest.

"Sorry," he mutters. "Sorry." His eyes redden.

"What's your name?" I whisper.

I don't have to tell him mine, which is etched on a pin jabbed in my apron.

"Jerry." His tremor tells me it's the truth.

"You need some help, Jerry?"

"No." He shakes his head longer than he needs to. "No. Some things … you can't take back."

I fall back a step, and Jerry gives me a feeble smile. He's talking as if he killed someone, but those hands could only close around a bottle's neck. Jerry's meanness is weak and sudden, exhausted in a spurt. Maybe he cheated on his wife. He'd never fight her if she threw him out. Whatever he's done, it's made him feel as if he's a piece of filth marring the earth. It takes something pretty bad to make you feel that you don't deserve to eat.

Jerry reappears in that corner each morning, as though the currents of the room had washed him there. He stares up at the TV as if it were a tree branch changing slowly from day to day. The Haverford bathrooms have showerheads like sunflowers, but he can't have stood under the one he's paying for. Like his stubble, the reek of him is pushing its way out. He fills the air with bitter oiliness like a man living on the street.

The Haverford guests have bubbles around them, spaces where you can't poke or touch. Technically they share the breakfast room, but they drift through it alone. A rule of their universe says that things can flow out of their bubbles but not in. When a blackening slice wedges itself in the toaster, they can ask me for help, but I can't offer it. As I learned in training, I should be ready to assist but never tell people what to do. Jerry's sludgy smell makes his bubble grow, so that he's taking up too much space. Even in that back corner, his stink jostles people as they walk by. They turn and sniff, unable to believe that unwashed smell has invaded their green breakfast room. But in one respect, he's like the others: if he wants my help, he'll ask for it.

One morning, he just isn't there. His corner seat calls him, and the TV misses his gaze. I ask the housekeepers if they've seen him, and they know straight off who I mean.

"A pig," says a round-faced woman with gray hair. "Good riddance."

They haven't found any bottles in his room, and they don't know where he's gone.

Without Jerry, I realize how tired I feel as I slog my way through the days. I get up at four and jolt into high gear when I unlock the kitchen at five. Breakfast starts at six, but hairy-legged guests in shorts peer in hungrily at five thirty. From seven to nine I fill coffee urns, rescue smoking toast, capture escaped flakes. By ten I've wiped down the waxy tables and locked away the tempting food.

When I climb the dirt path to the Run-Rite Inn, cars zoom by with morning zeal. Luz gives me the rooms of the last to check out, the most miserable slobs. People who have to be on the road by six treat their rooms the way soldiers treat a camp. They're in and out like a charged-up cowboy who hasn't seen a girl in months. The ones who leave two minutes before checkout have pushed themselves into every drawer. They pee in the shower and wallow in bed because no one down the road wants to see them. Scouring them from the rooms takes a wrestler's arms and more time than Luz will allow. When I get done at six, I float down the path like a bottle bobbing down a muddy river. I drift up and down the Dollar World aisles, quivering under the blue fluorescent lights. I choose some noodle soup and Mallomars for supper, then fall asleep halfway through *Forensic Team*. No matter what I do, I always slip off before the killer is found.

9

One morning I emerge to find the strip dead. A lonely truck growls its way between gray buildings a shade darker than the dawn. Without power, our strip is an inert thing that serves only to catch tumbleweeds. The silence tightens my flesh as though someone were turning a screw. I miss the green voice of the Dollar World sign buzzing away on its post. I didn't know what a friend that hum was to me in my quick walks through the dark. Without it, the taps of my feet call out to anyone who can hear. In this blackness, anything could happen. A shadow shifts in the doorway of Never-Ending Nails, and I sprint for the Haverford.

Carl, the manager, has jammed the doors open, since they have lost the power to slip apart. He could be Jake's father, except that his suit hangs so naturally I can't imagine his flesh. Carl reins in his voice as he issues orders about refueling a generator. The Haverford can make power when it needs to, but someone has forgotten to buy gas. Carl starts when he sees me and covers his phone.

"No breakfast today. We can't risk it."

"But I could put out some bread, maybe some fruit."

"No. The refrigerators have been down since two. You want to poison these people?"

I stand rooted in the spooky lobby lit by a flashlight and

a guttering candle. Carl must have taken the candle from the housekeepers' break room, where it warms a picture of a black-eyed soldier.

Arrow loses power anytime our line breaks, a slender loop from Pinto to Jones City. On the necklace dangling from Vegas to Norfolk, we hang as the weakest strand. In this part of the country, no trees tear the wires, but anything that moves can short them out. We've been left in the dark by drunken truckers, charred birds, and one angry loner trying to tap the line. It's amazing that we can survive at all, but so far, the power has always come back with no apology for having left us.

Carl frowns and jerks his chin toward me as though trying to shake me loose. "Don't punch in. We don't need you today. We should have our power back tomorrow. You can come back then."

I hate to walk out into the gray silence, but there's nothing else I can do. In their rooms, the Haverford guests are sleeping, and those with uncharged phones will dream on. They don't know that for the past four hours, they've been lying in black, silent cells. I think the stillness would wake me, the hushing of the room's noisy breath. Once peeps arouse those toned people, the dead rooms around them will give a shock. They fell asleep looking forward to light but will be greeted by coffin walls. Only waffles will calm them, and any minute now they'll be appearing, stiff and loud. Maybe it's just as well Carl doesn't want me. For now, he stands alone, lit on one side by a fading beam and on the other by a flickering Virgin.

When the strip goes dead, the Run-Rite Inn sometimes keeps its power, since Frontage Road is on a different spur.

Whether they've gone dark or not, Jake could use my help. The Merrill Highway has brightened a shade so that the buildings form dark shapes against the sky. As each car approaches, I hold my breath until its lights have passed. At the Roundabout Inn, shirts hang draped from a railing, limp but too weary to fall. Jerry might be staying in there, but I've seen no sign of him. I hope he kicks free of what's gripping him because I hate to see a person squeezed.

Over Frontage Road, the blue Run-Rite Inn sign hums as though it hasn't heard the world is dark. Jake must have come on at six, since his voice warms the grayness as he speaks to the driver of a white van. The long-haired man keeps his eyes on Jake, but the Asian girl in the passenger seat stares as if I were an angel in the dark. She looks as though she wishes she were me out here walking across the lot. Seeing me has never given anyone joy, and no one has envied me before. Under the force of her eyes, I freeze. She rises in a spasm, then falls back as the white van rolls. Jake hits the side twice, a heartbeat, whump-*bump*.

"You know those people?"

Jake turns with a start. The light spilling from the office doesn't reach his eyes, but his blink clears a flash almost like fear.

"Ginny? What are you doing here?"

"Power's out. Carl sent me away."

Jake squints down the hill as though seeing for the first time that Arrow is a bowl of gray. Jake lives thirty miles east in Pinto, a town with a Walmart and multiplex. He should have missed Arrow's glow on the way in, but on these plains, it barely stirs the night even at its brightest.

Jake gropes for his phone. "I'd better tweet that we have power."

"Anyone driving by will see our sign," I say. "Who were those people?"

Jake glances up and smiles. "Oh, he's just a good guy. Fun to talk to."

"That girl riding with him sure was pretty."

Her look is twisting my insides. She wanted to be in my stumpy body instead of the lovely one she has. Jake steps into the light so that I can't tell whether the brightness on his face comes from inside or outside.

"Yeah, his girlfriend's a beauty. Good thing you're here. We'll fill today if they don't get their power back downtown."

I stoop to pick up a tissue crushed into the shape of a popcorn kernel.

"Luz will be here at seven. She can put you to work."

Jake's grin deepens as he studies me, his phone hanging at his side. "It's nice to see you. I've missed you mornings. You care about this place."

While Jake sends messages bragging about our power, I prowl the brightening lot. At its edge, a plastic bag lies spread-eagled across some sage. Into it I drop flattened bottles and foil sticky with red sauce. I pocket a quarter that gleams at me like a staring silver eye. My bag fills quickly with squashed cups and newspapers flapping against tires. I feel as though I'm harvesting a field to feed the hungry jaws of the dumpster.

As I peel back a flyer from a wheel, Spanish spills into the warming air. Luz, Marielena, and Pili have arrived, dropped by a friend on her way to work. Their hair shines in the electric light, even the black streak of Pili's roots. With no power in the trailer park, they haven't eaten or washed, but they have come early to work. Luz moves as though trying to shake off her stickiness.

"¡Mira, que 'stá la chata!" cries Pili.

Luz silences her with a glare. I clutch the swollen bag and a handful of gritty paper.

"Hey, Ginny. No Haverford today? No breakfast for the gringos?"

Jake opens the office door, and a sweet smell spills out. Triumphantly he raises a pot of coffee.

"Breakfast is on me. Ginny! Go raid Janet."

Jake sets the coffee on a concrete bench and hands me a wad of singles. I scrub the grease and dust from my hands while Luz and Pili crowd the bathroom mirror, pulling their faces and applying makeup. Marielena hovers behind them, angling for a spot.

Janet stands in the breezeway, her riches gripped in silver coils. A grill of metal behind her glass protects her from looting fists. In her bottom row hang honey buns extending back into the dark. One by one I feed in Jake's dollars, and her silver spirals turn. The buns land with soft crackles, each package rejoicing to fall free. As the sun turns shadows into hard-edged things, we devour sticky sweetness.

Not many people have checked out, so Luz pairs me with Marielena. All those honey buns have made us sleepy, and Mari glances at the mussed bed as if she wants to climb into it. Close your eyes, and a bed will glide off like a magic raft bearing you to bliss. The bluebird sleeves of Mari's Run-Rite Inn shirt hang dully against her brown arms. In that spangly blue dress, Marielena shone, but she needs reds to make her lips glow. With gestures, I guide her to the far side of the bed, and we shake the sheets and pull them tight. Mari smiles as she strokes the smooth cotton, revealing teeth pointy as a cat's. I toss the bedspread into place, and my shirt pulls free from my jeans. Mari freezes, her eyes on my blistered skin.

"It's nothing." I try to keep my voice smooth. "That happened long ago. Everything's fine now."

Together we tuck the spread around the pillows as though we were hiding two hoarded buns. Mari's hand strokes the quilted surface, unwilling to leave it.

"I wonder who this woman is." I try to soothe her with my voice.

A rare thing at the Run-Rite Inn, a woman staying more than one night. Our guest's soft nightgown hangs next to folded slacks, the property of a commanding body. This woman is big, but she's arranged her things as though she likes to fill up space. Her bottles and tubes stand like bowling pins waiting for a ball to roll across the counter. On the nightstand, her remote control lies parallel to a book with a bare-chested man on the cover. He's staring at a woman in a low-cut gown as though he'll die if he can't grab her. A hair lies curled among the remote's black buttons, short and fine but too gray to hide. I bet this woman is selling something. She must have come in last night, and she's been looking forward to pancakes in syrup before showing her catalogues to the dollar stores. If she has a healthy travel budget, she's staying here so that she can pocket the rest. When she finds the restaurants dark, will she wait for power or head on down I-50? She has poised those pants so that they balance exactly and mean to hang a good, long time. Any minute now, she may come back to grab a honey bun and coffee.

I form a wedge with my thumbs and fingers to show Mari that when she wipes the counter, the bottles should go back in the same shape. She hesitates before the mirror, discovering surprises in her stray-cat face. For a girl under twenty, Mari has blotchy skin, with spots that look like they've been smacked. Her hand creeps toward the foremost bowling pin, a silver-topped vial of eye cream. I shake my head, but the corners of her mouth harden. She unscrews the cap and looks into a gleaming valley. The click of that heavy cap against the counter speaks of a balm from another world.

"Let me show you," I whisper. "Don't stick your finger in. Just brush the edge, so she can't see."

Kaitlin lost her job stealing makeup, but moonfaced Kaitlin was never too bright. An angry blonde woman showed Jake the jar, defiled by a finger-shaped crater. Jake sent for Kaitlin and fired her while the woman nodded with satisfaction. The look on Kaitlin's face told him everything, like an iceberg splitting in pieces.

"For a finger full of thirty-dollar grease," he told me. "Who gives up a good job for that? Decent people stay here. We can't go poking into their things."

I touch my pinky to the valley's edge and raise it to Marielena's cheek. She closes her eyes and breathes out slowly as I rub cream into her cool skin. Barely breathing myself, I massage each rough place, and she smiles like a baby being soaped. I tilt the vial until bluish light blasts the valley, which has broadened. I have left no telltale gouges, nothing to complain about. This woman will think her cream's just vanishing, melting away as everything does.

The door bumps the loaded cart propping it, and

Marielena's cry hits the mirror like a bird. Jake is pushing his way in around the cart. With a quick twist, I secure the silver lid and restore the vial to the triangle's tip.

"Power's back."

Jake's big body takes over the room in a way that no one else's can. He glances at the bright counter and nods.

"Who's up front?" I ask.

People will be checking out. Jake must have wanted to tell someone pretty bad.

"Frank."

Jake grimaces, then smiles at the sexy book placed with military precision on the nightstand. I gesture to Mari to spray the shower while I polish the faucet and sink.

"So I guess we won't fill, huh?" I ask.

"We might. No stampede, though." Disappointment is slowing Jake's moves.

When he can, Jake likes to look in on us when we clean. He says that he wants to know about the rooms, but I think he gets lonely in the office, even with his computer world. He approaches until the blasting blue light catches him. It bleaches his curly hair, his round face, his thick arms. His hands test the bars of the clothes rack and shift the suspended hangers. The light steals his eyes' color but not their strength as they shift to Marielena. With her hands over her head, she scrubs in quick strokes. My hands move in circles when I scour, but hers dart back and forth like a dog on a short chain. Jake's lips part as he watches her black ponytail brushing the jeans below her blue shirt.

"Good work, you two."

Marielena turns, gripping her sponge. Her flushed face is bright, and the overhead lights make her black eyes gleam.

"Bueno!" Jake raises his voice. "Limpia … limpia como ella." His warm hand pats my shoulder. "Anything she does, you do."

Mari's lips tighten, but her laugh breaks through. Jake has been trying to learn Spanish, and Luz, Pili, and Mari laugh in splutters when they hear his sounds. Jake's Spanish wanders in numb, slow steps like a man out of his mind on drugs. I don't even try to speak Spanish, but I can understand their digs at Jake. He grins at Mari, who has raised a lean arm to brush black tendrils from her forehead. The damp is forming dark roses on her shirt where it clings to her hot skin.

Jake leans against the counter and motions for Mari to work. I wish just once he would look at me the way he stares at her swinging ponytail. Jake tries so hard to be professional that he never mentions a girlfriend. He doesn't strike me as Manny's kind of guy, and he looks at girls like he wants to swallow them. Luz said a friend of hers saw him in Pinto with a white girl so hot she could almost pass for Mexican. I think he's holding out for the girl with the iPad that we saw in that college ad. Someone rich and smart, maybe from a family that could loan him money for his first motel. For now, he's dealing with his hunger, and he won't go prodding Mari the way some bosses do. His voice set off a wave in my belly when he called that girl in the van a beauty.

"Where were they going?" I ask. "That long-haired guy and the Chinese girl?"

"Vietnamese," says Jake. His eyes catch mine, and I find spots of green the lights haven't bleached. "They were headed for Wichita. They have to travel for a business they run."

"Ever seen them before?"

Jake rubs the back of his head and stares at the bowling pin bottles.

"Yeah ..." His voice slows as tries to recollect. "They've stayed here a few times. We're the best deal in a hundred miles."

He smiles as a thought breaks through. "Ginny, you know what you should do? You should go back down to the Haverford."

"But Carl sent me away."

I rub a stray drop from the faucet. Jake said he liked having me back. What did I do to change his mind?

"Yeah, I know. That guy can be a real asshole. I've heard they sent him here to punish him after he screwed up in Dallas. But if you went back—it would show him you cared. People will want refunds if there's no breakfast, and he's not going to cook it."

With a heave of my stomach, I picture the nest of anger into which Jake is pushing me. Mari climbs from the tub, and Jake and I look in to inspect. Not a single hair breaks the white gleam.

"Marielena's got this," says Jake. "Why don't you go help Carl and come back when you're done? Come on, I'll walk down with you."

He smiles at Mari, who shrinks when she sees that I'm leaving.

"Bueno," says Jake. "Limpia más."

The last thing I hear from the room is a tiny snicker.

Sunlight is baking the balcony, and I narrow my eyes against its force. Following the shadow of Jake's bulk, I make my way to the office. Frank pushes himself up with skinny arms, his eyes warming with relief. He hates to work up front and prefers uncomplaining machines to jumpy people with questions. He frowns at me as if I were a thundercloud darkening the sky at the wrong hour.

"Hey, I thought she got another job." Frank looks questioningly at Jake.

If it were up to Frank, I'd disappear altogether, since I give him most of his work. Every day, I tell him about curling plastic, running toilets, anything leaky, anything loose. Without me, he would float through his days until water crashed from the pipes.

"This is Ginny," says Jake. "Ginny, our housekeeper? You can talk to her."

"Sorry." Frank scowls at sticky plastic pushing its way from the trash. "Hey, you guys ate all the honey buns."

Jake motions for Frank to leave the desk as if he were whisking him loose.

"Go check Janet."

"I did. She looks like a plague of locusts came through."

With the power out, Janet must have supplied breakfast to everyone at the Run-Rite Inn, plus a few smart people who walked up the hill.

"You'd better get back down there," Jake tells me. "If there's no breakfast, those people will tear the place up."

His first idea made more sense: the Haverford guests would want refunds. To Carl, paying them would be like ripping the green drapes from their rods and throwing the toaster through the glass window. I slip out as Jake settles at his computer, checking for tracks Frank might have left. He won't find any. Frank moves through the online world as he moves through this one, gliding silently as a fish.

A hoot cuts through the dryers' roar, and I make a

detour to the laundry. Pili is laughing openmouthed, biting the hot air with chipped teeth. She rests a palm on each broad thigh like a sumo wrestler waiting to be charged. Luz faces her, arms spread, her eyes glowing and her cheeks puffed out. I wonder if they're imitating Jake's last attempt to speak Spanish. Could Mari already have slipped down here and told them? Pili spots me in the doorway, and all the fun leaves her face. Luz turns to me but keeps her smile.

"Hey, Ginny."

I don't like the way she says my name, "Chinny," as if I were a Dollar World toy.

"What's happening?" I ask.

"I was talking about my kid Rafa. He loves the wind, and when it's blowing hard, he screams to go out."

Luz spreads her arms to show me how her boy tries to grab the wind. She forms a circle with her arms as though she were gathering plants, but her armful of stalks melts away. Pili glances at me, then erupts. Luz keeps her going with a melody of Spanish over the dryers' bass.

"I have to lock him in," says Luz. "He keeps trying to run after the wind. He chases clouds. 'Come back!' he yells—not like he's asking them, like he's *telling* them. Once he got as far as the church."

Pili frowns and offers a stream of advice. Not a pretty prospect, a kid running loose. If a truck doesn't flatten him, some guy might grab him and deal him a worse fate.

"Who's watching him now?" I ask.

Luz blows a stream of air from the corner of her mouth. "Linda. She watches all our kids down there while we work."

I try to imagine kids, warm, sticky things who hug your legs when they're happy and kick you when they're not.

Little things that are always there, wanting what they can't have and screaming when they don't get it. I wonder how Linda controls a whole trailer full with only a TV and a box of cookies. Luz has two boys, Rafael—known as Rafa—and a younger one, and she never mentions their father. No wonder Rafa chases the wind when she and Linda are the only grown-ups he knows.

Luz and Pili have lost their smiles and are scanning me with strange stares. I don't know how I do this to people, shut off the light in their eyes.

"Sorry," I say. "I just wanted to know. I'm glad he's okay."

"Yeah, he's doing great."

Luz's dark eyes push me out the door and into the blazing sunlight.

10

Carl smiles broader than I thought he would, so that crinkles form around his brown eyes. He releases his breath as though he missed me the minute the lights came back on.

"Jake sent me back. He thought you'd need me."

"'Preciate it." Carl nods.

His beard is poking its way out as though every bristle wants to leave him. The housekeepers' candle has deadened in its glass tube, and my hand closes over the painted Virgin.

"You want me to take this back?"

"Yeah, yeah." Carl waves his hand as if he could toss it back to the altar.

The bony woman with the kid in Afghanistan will be upset to find her candle burned. On break she sucks glowing cigarettes while the Virgin shines on her son's face. Those candles with the lady floating in gold daggers cost five dollars, and I doubt Carl is going to pay her back. He checks his thin black strip of a watch.

"Shit, almost eight. I put a girl in there, but she doesn't know what she's doing. Tell her you're taking over and she should go clean."

Carl smiles at an old couple ambling up, each hauling a red plastic suitcase.

"Is the breakfast ready now?" asks the wife, her voice rising with hope.

The thick-necked girl Carl has put in charge is delighted to run free. Once she's gone, tall, taut people circle me like famished coyotes. The empty fruit bowl and yogurt case call, but I can't break through the ring of stabbing eyes. A gray-haired man in running shorts tries to catch my eyes, but I watch the hairs rise on his lean legs.

"Miss, I see you're all alone here. Why don't you do the coffee first?" he says.

Behind me a woman keeps starting to talk and then stifling her own voice. "If ... if you could just ..."

Fingers peck my shoulder. I cry out. The bodies in the circle jump back.

"Let her work," orders the man in shorts. "Set priorities." His gray eyes sweep the room as though he were taking a building in Iraq.

The circle breaks, and I run to the pantry. Bread, bagels, and pastries first. God help me if they stick in the toaster. Each time I dart into the room with supplies, voices and fingers swirl around me. Each voice prods, trying to drive me from my path into a hollow where I will serve its owner alone. I keep my eyes free, and in my mind, I kill the monsters one by one. I align the bagels in perfect rows and snuff out the voices burning my neck.

They're not here, I keep telling myself. *No one is here.*

I dodge the noisy bodies and see only the frightened shelves begging to be filled. The coffee urn in the lobby is dry, although its brown liquid was lukewarm. As I pour a brown torrent from a silver can, people hover as if they could shame me into moving faster. Ten eyes are staring at each finger.

"I can't believe this. I stayed here for the breakfast," mutters a fat woman in light blue sweats.

"She's doing the best she can. I think it's just her," murmurs her silver-haired husband.

The lady in the gray suit never said what to tell Haverford guests when the lights go out. I slop canned fruit into the plastic bowl and shove apples into the yogurt case. Carl has ordered me to throw every yogurt in the refrigerator straight into the dumpster. He peeps in as I'm filling glass bowls with pink, blue, and yellow packets. He frowns, then catches my eye and nods. Not many people could walk into this storm without being blown apart.

It takes the Haverford breakfast room weeks to recover from that morning without power. The forest-green curtains hang tense, bracing themselves for a pull. The toast creeps nervously, conscious that the coils above it could lose their orange glow. Breakfast flies like a kite on a gusty day, ready to take a plunge. I move through the room replenishing, rubbing, trying to show that even if the power goes, I won't. With time, the curtains relax their weave, and the waffle iron turns without wincing.

I am wiping each table with four quick strokes when breath stirs the hairs on my arm. The thick-necked girl from the day without power is standing next to me, unsmiling.

"Carl," she says simply.

My stomach feels like the rag clenched in my hand. Carl's office has a wooden door that can close, unlike Jake's open space behind the desk. Dark shelves stacked with papers line Carl's walls, but his desk sits like a stone block that only a bulldozer could move.

"Have a seat." Carl inclines his hand as though inviting me to slide down a chute. I settle and grip the waxy cushion with both hands.

"I'm taking you off breakfast," he says.

My breath catches, and my eyes sting so that I shift them to the window. A skinny drifter with a shock of brown hair is swinging his way across the lot.

"Has someone complained?"

"Yeah." Carl's brown eyes try to snag mine and pull them back. "A whole bunch from that day we lost power. You show up on time, treat the equipment well. You're clean. It's …"

If I look at him, a levee will break. I know what the trouble is. For breakfast, people want a pretty girl the way they want crinkly carnations on their tables. A face that looks smashed by an angry hand doesn't help your eggs slide down easily. Just once I'd like to hear someone say it.

"What's the trouble?" I murmur.

"The trouble is, you won't goddamn look at me when you talk to me," says Carl. "You creep people out. That's what they say—you won't look at them. They're posting comments online: 'unfriendly staff in the breakfast room.' That day without power, you got the food out fast, but you didn't give them what they really wanted."

"What's that?" My voice lies flat with edges like a sheet of metal.

"Talk to them! Smile, make a joke! Tell them you're on it, everything's fine!"

My eyes snap back to find Carl leaning forward. Black

hair rises from each joint of his fingers. I draw a breath but can't speak.

"Aw, man." Carl shakes his head, one long swipe each way, as though trying to rub something out. "I hate this place. The Mexican girls are gorgeous, but they don't speak English. The others are meth heads and crack whores. You're none of those things. You're the best worker I've had—but not for breakfast."

"Why not? I like breakfast."

My voice surprises me, strong and full. If Carl's going to fire me, at least I will have fought. I won't have to lie in bed and think I let him toss me like a tissue.

Carl leans back and folds his hands across his stomach. "Look, you were trained. What's the first thing they taught you? People come here for the breakfast. They hate to get up in the morning. They want a pretty, smiling face to say, 'Hi, how're you doing?'—to make them feel someone's glad they're alive. You've got to talk to people!"

"I talked to Jerry," I say.

"Who's … Oh, Jesus, that psycho? Housekeeping said you were asking about him. You talked to him, of all people?"

"What happened to him?" I blurt. "Did you throw him out?"

"I should have." Carl glares at the window, and his eyes return to me, recharged. "He left when his credit card maxed out. That guy needs a loony bin, not a motel."

I sit unmoving against his stare.

"Look, I need someone on breakfast who's friendly," he says. "Don't you ever smile? I've watched you, and it's like you're working for the room. Those people in there need someone on their side—someone to make sure their waffle turns out nice when their life sucks."

"When do you want me to go?" I murmur.

"Oh, I'm not firing you!" Carl's voice is suddenly too loud. "I want you on housekeeping. Jake says you're an ace. You could make more here than you do there. People down here leave tips."

The thought of soft dollars left by pudgy hands repulses me more than stacks of pizza boxes.

"Housekeeping's the right job for you, and you should do it," says Carl, rising. "You're good at it. You think about coming on full time, okay?"

"Yeah," I tell him. "I will."

"Let me know in a week," he says. "The offer's good until then."

On the way out, I pause before the breakfast room. The sugar bowls stand impassive, but the waffle iron leers.

I never liked you, it says. *So long, chata.*

11

There come days of wind so strong it tries to tear Arrow from its roots. Sheets of insulation spin from roofs and cartwheel across the Merrill. White plastic bags soar free, only to be flattened against walls. Signs crash to the ground, and tumbleweeds fly as if they were whirling through open desert. The blast tests every securing nail, and many are found wanting.

When I walk, I narrow my eyes to slits and shield them with my left arm. I pump with my right to pull me through the air, which is full of grit and loose grass. By the time I reach the Run-Rite Inn, a hundred tendrils have pulled free from my braid. My ears are coated with dust. Even though I've kept my mouth shut, grit grinds between my teeth.

I don't know how Luz is controlling Rafa, who must want to soar into every gust. I can feel him longing to fly and follow the wind wherever it goes. Luz looks battered and angry because she's anchored to the earth. Whipped hair brings out her fighting spirit, as if the world's hand were mussing her.

"Ginny!" she says in exasperation. "I'll knock two rooms off your quarter if you take the *golosos*."

Golosos are eaters, and they can torture a room worse than druggies or drunks. Few people who stay at the

Run-Rite can afford drugs, or if they buy them, they can't afford a motel. But at the Pinto Walmart or the Jones City Sam's Club, you can buy tubs of popcorn, fleets of cookies, sacks of candy. Not many pleasures compare to that: lying warm under the covers, watching *Forensic Team* with your food laid out as if you were a queen. The cookies stand waiting in plastic trays, and you empty the rows one by one. Crisp sweetness, crisp saltiness in your mouth, as much as you want for as long as you want. Everything depends on your reaching hand—which bite to swallow, which channel to watch. At some point you wake up in a gritty bed surrounded by what you didn't want.

I understand the golosos better than the drunks, but I would never treat a room like these eaters do. I take Luz's deal because no one else can save 210 from these monsters begging rats and cockroaches to invade. Hairs twining in the drain tell me these two were women: one with a frizzy brown head; the other with short dark hair; both fond of mango shampoo. What they've devoured in one night amazes me: golden Doritos, rainbow cupcakes, mint Oreos. At some point they ordered pizzas, because two boxes stand gaping open, greasy skins fused to their roofs. They must have been throwing jelly beans, since I hold my own private Easter egg hunt, seeking flashes of color along the walls. Cinnamon red, lime green, lavender grape. I sample an orange bean wedged into a corner and squeeze sunshine between my teeth. No amount of shaking can free the sheets from salty brown triangles and black crumbs. Like most eaters, these two took nothing with them, as if they were ashamed of the memory. The clear trash bags won't hold their debris, so I mash the rest into the pizza boxes.

The instant I step from the room, the wind catches me like bandits robbing a loaded coach. I clutch the boxes, propping the top with my chin, but the trash bags rise, trying to pull free. My feet find their own way down the stairs as the bags pummel me on both sides. Across the lot sits the green dumpster, guarding our trash from the marauding wind. An American flag brightens its side, and its green ears stiffen as I approach. Once a week, a roaring truck rams a fork through these loops to hoist it and empty it out.

Today its black plastic lid is closed, and wind sucks angrily at the cracks. Not that it contains much loot, but people jump in to root among the bags. Thin drifters in hoodies and torn jeans rip through the plastic skins to find food. Mothers and kids from the wooden houses in town come with carts on a regular circuit. Most are hunting bottles to redeem, but they also come for the thrill. People driving I-50 leave trash from all over, collapsed alligators from the Galveston Pleasure Pier, canvas bags from conventions in Vegas. They toss strings of blue beads from New Orleans and squashed cowboy hats from Dodge City. Patch this loot up, and it feeds fantasies. Some lands in the downtown antique shops. I leave my goodies on top so that no one hungry will have to dig for them.

I set down my load to raise the lid, and wind blasts open the top box. Paper and plastic explode into the sage. I heave everything I can into the dumpster and run chasing after the rest. Napkins scatter like butterflies as if I were a scientist trying to pin them. With empty hands, I rush back to lower the lid. I boost myself onto the dumpster's green rim and inhale the sick, sour stench.

The trash is heaving, and I freeze with my arm extended. Sometimes stray cats dive in, but they couldn't make the stuffed bags shiver like this. A cardboard box is quaking as something scratches its way to the top. The flaps part, and a black-eyed girl stares at me, her eyes wild in her thin face. Her long black hair is sticky with sickening juice from some bag.

"Cứu em! Làm ơn mà chị!" she cries.

I can't tell whether these are words or sounds. Fiercely she grips the cardboard flaps.

"Làm ơn! Em chết mất!"

She pushes herself up, and gleams catch the sun. She is wearing a black-and-blue sequin dress.

I drop from the rim and try to breathe. She looks like that girl in the van but younger—a scared little kid.

"Kids keep you from starting fresh," said Mom.

She didn't know I could hear her through the wall. I used to hear everything, the thumping, the gasping. For a while she and Harper liked to laugh when they were done.

"Yeah," said Harper, "kids are turds you can't flush."

Mom laughed in heaves that made the mattress squeak.

"How'd you ever hook up with such an ugly bastard?" asked Harper. "She sure as hell don't look like you."

I never saw my dad, but I always pictured a monster ramming a baby into my mom that she pushed back out.

"Oh, I guess I'm just a magnet for ugly."

Mom used to toss words like that before Harper knocked them out of her. His words hit hers like pool balls that drove her down into the corner pockets. *Ugly* was his word. *Bedtime. Discipline.* Each look at me reminded him that my dad got to my mom first. Mom said that Harper was a good earner and more fun than a road race in a hot Porsche. When Harper came home, she used to twist in curves like a cat until he pinned her down. Then he would spot me watching him.

Most of all, Harper hated to see me chew.

"Just look at those jaws working," he said. "Like some goddamn little termite nymph."

Harper laid flooring, and he couldn't stand the bugs that turned his joists to dust.

Most of the time I could disappear. I could sit right across from him at the table as long as I didn't raise my eyes. I just kept mine on my chili, three beans to a spoon until only red paste lined the bowl.

"You're some little eater," said Harper. "You look at me when I talk to you."

Harper liked me to look when he spoke but otherwise not at all. He had curly red-brown hair and skin that glowed when he ate his fill. He held his shoulders straight, but his arms rested on the table. One of them caught my chin and tilted my head back until he had my eyes. He held me there pinched, each rough breath pushing my face up and down just a hair.

"What are you doing?" Mom's voice sounded too high.

Harper breathed out slowly, and his fingers tightened.

"I'm looking for any sign of you. You sure she's yours?"

Mom looked from me to Harper. "That's not funny."

"Oh, I think it is."

He leaned back and folded his arms behind his head.

"The hottest woman in the state has a termite nymph? Look at your mom. Aren't you ashamed? How many bowls of chili you just eat?"

Mom was long and thin in the middle, and no one knew where the food went. She was always twisting, turning, and men loved to grab her and hold her still.

"There's a monster lives down in that sink," said Harper. "You know what he likes to eat?"

Harper's eyes turned golden brown. "Fat little girls' fingers. Gobbles them down like chicken nuggets."

"Harper," said Mom, "don't tell her that."

Harper rose up. "Oh, it's the truth."

His hand closed on my wrist, and he pulled me toward the sink. He flicked a switch, and the monster chugged to life. I scrabbled, a stuffed thing struggling to twist loose. Harper's free hand slammed the side of my head and turned my ear to a bar of heat. Mom yelped like a puppy. Harper pulled my hand toward the black flower of flaps.

"That monster will chew your fingers off. Your grubby hand will be a mess of flying blood."

The monster snarled, and I hid my fingers in a tight fist. I pulled back, but my knuckles were parting the flaps. The growls were shredding my screams.

"Em sợ!" cries the girl in the box. She claws back her hair and reaches out.

Luz could never talk to this girl, and a twist in my stomach tells me not to tell Jake. With my heart slamming its way from my chest, I heave myself back up. I've never seen anyone so afraid, and I can't leave her here. I want to grab her by the wrist and run, but any path out of here is lined with a thousand eyes. Whoever she's hiding from would hear in no time of a fat woman in a blue T-shirt and a thin girl in a blue dress streaking down the Merrill Highway. I put my finger to my lips and raise my hands, palms down, telling her to stay put. She couldn't have found a better hiding place, down there under all that stench. I point to the pizza, cookies, and chips and bring my hand to my mouth.

"Hide," I say. "I'm going to get help."

I keep my eyes on hers, hoping that she can read them even though she doesn't understand a word.

12

I don't punch the clock, and as I duck out, I realize that Jake could fire me. He wouldn't want to, but corporate could make him, and I can't tell him about this frightened girl. The whump of his hand against that white van has been sounding in my head like a drum. Whoever she's hiding from, he knows them, and I'm afraid to think how. I pick my way around the back, where Luz and Mari are calling from room to room. As they clean, they cry to each other like birds in two trees, comparing their views of the world.

I reach the dirt path without being seen, but it seems to lengthen with each step. It must be a hundred degrees in that dumpster. If that girl's stifling in a box, why didn't I bring her water? How long will it be until she's missed? How long before the order comes to search the place from sticky roof to cracked floors? My lump of a stomach knows who will get that call: "Lost one. Find her, or else."

On a Roundabout balcony, a stringy-haired woman draws on a cigarette and stares. I'm not much to look at, but to her starved eyes, I'm a feast. Not many people pass this way on foot. I dodge her gaze, since if she knew who to call, she'd sell me for a five-dollar bag of meth. My breaths come quicker, and on the concrete sidewalk, my steps lengthen.

The bells of Never-Ending Nails clunk as if they were betraying an escaped cow.

"How are you?" cries Heather. "You early today! You get a day off, or they fire you?"

She laughs loudly, and I realize I've rushed down here with no idea what to say. Up close, Heather is a woman of fifty, double chin, strong arms, shrewd eyes. Gray threads give her hair an elegance I have never heard in her jarring voice. Her laugh fades, and her eyes narrow as she senses the trouble I've brought to her shop.

"There's a girl in a dumpster," I say.

I can feel the girl's breaths in that hot, stinking dark.

"A girl in a dumpster? What kind of girl?" Heather brings her puffy hands to the counter.

"Like you," I say. "Like her." I jerk my chin toward Judy, who has slipped from the back room to hear.

"Vietnamese girl?" Heather's voice sharpens. A pink jewel on her finger shoots light.

I nod.

"How you know she not Chinese? Or Thai? Why you come here and tell us?" Her eyes have gone hard and dark.

"Because … because you can talk to her. I think she's Vietnamese."

Heather breathes out slowly and shakes her head. Her black eyes are searing me. I follow the band of green around the walls and count the six empty black thrones. Judy creeps closer but freezes when Heather calls out sharply. She mutters what can only be a curse.

"You know what you doing? Who she hiding from? You try to help, they come look for you. Then they come for us. These people not stupid. She Vietnamese, this first place they look!"

"But you could talk to her. Find out who she is. Please! I can't tell her anything!"

My eyes sting, and my breaths roughen. Heather's eyes redden and swell. She sprays a stream of words at Judy, who nods, white and confused. With a growl, Heather ducks below the counter and rises with a pink purse and a water bottle. She nudges me toward the back, through a dark room that smells of pungent grease.

"Get down," she says as she starts a trembling green Dodge.

I duck, but I can't resist peeping out as the Haverford floats by. The strip flows past like a movie—Manny's shop, Dollar World, Scooter's Lounge. A thin woman walks, swinging her arms, and I recognize the smoker from the Roundabout. She must have raised enough to score a hit. Heather grimaces, as though guiding the wheel is taking all her strength. She mutters in a scolding way, and by the time she turns onto Frontage Road, she's glowering. I ask her to park between two cars, so that no one will notice our arrival. Quietly we creep toward the dumpster, sticky green in the searing sun. I heave up the lid, and Heather slips around back.

"Hello?" I whisper.

The plastic bags lie silently stuck. Either the girl is gone, or she's dead. Heather raps the metal and calls in a high-pitched cry. A weak voice answers, and the bags shudder. A huge carton rocks, and the girl appears at the top, red-eyed. Her face has shrunk since I saw it last.

"Cứu em! Em sợ quá!" she gasps.

Heather scolds fiercely. I heave myself up, and the girl pushes her way through the clinging bags. Her hand grips mine with a demon's strength, and in an instant she is standing between us, shaking in her sparkly dress. Its black skirt holds her from waist to midthigh, but her chest flashes indigo and aqua. She cries so shrilly that Heather claps a fat hand over her mouth. Together we pull her behind the dumpster, out of sight of the motel. The putrid air is making my stomach heave.

"What's she saying? What's 'em suh'?" I ask.

"Shut up," orders Heather. "She just say she scared."

"Can you help her?" I plead.

The girl stands rigid in her grip. Heather looks toward her car, and her face contorts.

"I take her now. Just for now, you hear? I can't keep her. You go back to work, so nobody say nothing. You see nothing, okay? You come down when you done."

"Thanks," I murmur, and she answers with a curse.

Heather and the escaped girl run for her car, bent as though a gunman on the roof had a bead on them and could shoot at any moment.

13

For the first time ever, I rival Luz in the race to get my rooms done. Thirteen of them, since Luz cut two and I've already sucked up the eaters' crumbs. None of the rooms will let me loose, like little kids pleading for their mother's care. Every one of them has been battered, as if the wind had infected people's spirits. One guy has covered a wall with footprints, using work boots of a small size. I feel as though the room has tilted and he's tromped all over its side. It's an accomplishment to leave any trace on those hard white peaks like plastic frosting. Maybe he was practicing a dance move where he had to run up the wall and flip. Or he wanted to see what tracks the boots left, so he'd always know which ones were his.

The sticky-daub wall shreds sponges like a grater, so I attack the prints strategically. The pink strawberry spray doesn't even faze them. While I bundle the sheets, they laugh at me in a chorus, dancing up and down like the man who left them. They don't know what I've got in my cart. When I dump the sheets, I grab my vegetable brush. I zap every print with green spray this time, and then I attack. The fine bristles enter every hollow, relishing the pale green foam. As my hand circles, the prints start to panic. I force foam into every one of them until their spirits break. Together they jeered at me, but now each one lies alone and terrified. One by one, I scour them to death. They die frightened, crying for mercy, begging to stay in the world. The green foam on the wall turns gray, and I use my most absorbent sponge as a blot. The slightest stroke would tear it to pieces. It takes me as long as I should spend on two rooms, but when I'm done, the wall shines like white-mountain frosting. You would never know that a man with small feet was trying to climb it all night.

He isn't the worst of the restless spirits who tormented my rooms last night. One woman shat in the tub and tried to force it down the drain. She probably thought she got away with it, but she left her stink on the steel cross support. Another "guest," desperate to pull something loose, peeled the caulk all the way around the counter. The most disgusting one left traces of herself all around the room for me to find. People do this sometimes to be remembered, leaving bits of themselves in the world. They plaster boogers onto cool metal hangers and wedge hair balls into the corners. To the bed frame they stick gum washed in their spit and chewed a thousand times by their teeth.

Luz looks in a little before three and catches me with my putty knife.

"¡Que la chingada!" she cries. "¡Apúrete! It's check-in time! They don't have to do brain surgery in there."

By six I have cleaned my last room, and my morning ride up the strip feels like a dream. As far as Luz knows, I'm slow because I'm crazy, not because I ran off for a girl.

I draw quick breaths as I walk down the slope, although at this hour, I belong here. With the wind at my back, I fly along, loose strands of hair whipping my face. Only one fat man watches from the Roundabout, defying the wind with his bulk.

I struggle with the door of Never-Ending Nails, and the bells clunk loudly. No one is in the shop, and the colors are communing. The lime-green band around the walls is urging the bottled tones to speak. I can almost hear their chatter when Heather emerges from the back room.

"Sit down," she says. "I do your nails. You sit like normal."

"I don't have any money," I say.

"That's okay. You give me another time."

Heather nudges me all the way back to Donna's favorite throne. I kick off my sandals and rest my feet on a white towel.

"How is she?" I ask.

Heather gathers her steel tools like a surgeon and won't answer until she's arranged them in the order she likes. She ties on a white mask, leaving only bright eyes crowded by puffs of skin.

"She can't stay here," she says.

A cool cotton pad drenched in chemicals attacks my circles of rose. The color disappears from the edges first. The white pad turns bloodred, and she tosses it aside. With expert jabs, she wipes the shrinking continents on my big toes and the pink rims around each nail. With a downward wave, she gestures for me to soak my feet, and she pulls off her mask.

"Just tell me how she's doing," I say.

Heather looks up with eyes weary but hard. "She better now. Eat, drink something. Won't stop talking. Finally she sleep. But she can't stay."

"Why not?" I grip the black plastic arms.

Heather's dark eyes defy the wrinkled flesh around them. "You don't know what you doing," she says. "These very bad people. She worth a lot. They kill to get her back. If they not find her, someone kill them."

"But how did she get here?" I ask. "Who is she? Does she have family?"

Heather hoists one foot from the tank and sets my heel down on the soft towel. She squints at a curved silver tool and holds it off to focus, then sets to work on my cuticles.

"Her family pay for her to come here. They pay part— the rest she work. These people tell her good job over here. Beauty job."

Pulses of pain mark her jabbing strokes.

"Like a model?" I ask.

"No, no! Like here—nail salon. But they lie."

"What's her name? How old is she?"

The pain travels from toe to toe as if a monster were biting them one by one. Heather snorts and shakes her head.

"She sixteen. Name Lành. I don't know why you do this. You got a good job. You could keep doing it your whole life."

Heather digs into the cuticles of my other foot, forcing them back from the nails. I wince at the burn of each jab.

"Could she stay here a few days? Until I find somewhere for her to go?"

"Where she go?"

The pulses of burning deepen.

"She speak no English, not allowed to work. She don't know nothing. Somebody got to take care of her."

Heather stops to study her work and reaches for her

silver nippers. Following her hand with her breath, she snips the white scraps of loose skin.

"Please. You must know somewhere she could go. Someplace with a lot of people like her—so she could work without anyone knowing."

I reach for her arm, but she shakes off my hand.

"Yeah. Vietnam." She chuckles as she grabs my other foot. "Safest place for her is where she come from."

I flex my toes, clean and wet and free to breathe.

"What if I help her?" I ask. "If I could keep her, find somebody to drive her—you know a place where she could go?"

"Boy, you don't quit!" She glares at my heels. "You in a hurry to be dead?"

I stare at the loops of philodendron leaves drinking the day's last light. A car eases into the spot near the door.

"Please!" I say. "These people don't know you. They don't know who you know. I could find her a ride. Just give me an address."

Heather stares down into the brown tank. Three jets on each side trouble the water.

"I got a cousin in Houston," she murmurs. "Lot of Vietnamese people there."

"Could she stay with your cousin? Maybe she could help out."

The bells clunk, and a heavyset woman enters with a determined step.

"Hello!" cries Heather brightly.

She signals for the customer to sit in the black throne nearest the front desk. In her language, she calls into the back room, and Judy emerges with a frightened look.

She's wearing her usual blue blouse and jeans, but her stiff movements tell me the runaway girl has been firing her imagination. Nervously, she smiles at the big customer in a sweatshirt and pants.

Heather squeezes pink lotion into her palm and massages it into my heels. Her rough touch makes my shoulders tense.

"What does your cousin do?" I ask suddenly.

"Trời đất ơi!" she cries. "My God! Where you think I send her? My cousin has a place like this. But in Houston, they give more tip."

As Judy bends over the fat woman's feet, her hair almost falls from its clip. Has she been lying down with Lành? How will Lành feel when she wakes up alone?

"Tell me the name—the address of your cousin's place," I say. "I can get her there."

Heather shakes her head, rises, and walks stiffly toward the register. The gray-haired customer glances up while pulling a book from her bag. Heather stops before the rack and squints until the customer sinks into her book. She slips to the desk and frowns as she writes, forming her letters carefully. Before she returns to me, she grabs a bottle from the rack.

"You didn't pick color," she says.

"You didn't ask me to." I wiggle my toes.

"You always pick pink," she says. "Wrong color for you."

Heather untwists the cap of a bottle of sparkling green.

14

Balboa Street dies slowly as you walk toward the edge of town. The asphalt dries, fades, and cracks until it breaks up into pebbles. By the time you reach the Bible church, it has crumbled into gravel. Any car that passes over it complains as its tires seek smooth ground. At the trailer park entrance, the gravel road softens into a dirt lane. "Private. No trespassing," say black signs tacked to the entrance posts. A blue-and-white arch crowns the entrance, saying "Mariposa Trailer Homes."

No one stops me as I trudge past the office, but even the smallest kid knows I don't belong. An orange cat raises his head and scowls at me with golden eyes. If I can't disappear in this place, Lành never could. I feel as though I've walked right into a ring of staring eyes. The unseen glances push me harder than the remnants of the wind. I can see its traces in Mariposa Park: plastic deer toppled, trash cans rolling, and a pair of striped boxer shorts that escaped from someone's clothesline.

The dirt entrance road loops into an oval with alleys linking the bottom and top. Trailers line the paths so closely that people have strung clotheslines between them. No two trailers look alike, and their personalities make me smile. Most are white, but every one has color. Blue curtains flutter as a hand releases them, and green plastic frogs guard a door.

Dead cars and wrecked swing sets steal some space, junk no one can afford to haul off. But each trailer looks as though someone cares for it. Two red wooden cardinals perch on one windowsill, pecking for imaginary seed.

I follow children's voices up an inner lane, where they are shouting in Spanish. They run in circles over hard-packed ground and reach out as though giving each other shocks. A tiny girl in a blue dress screams, and they laugh as I cover my ears.

"Luz?" I ask, and they giggle at this pale, pudgy thing that can't talk.

A tall boy with a broken brow points to a trailer on a corner lot.

"Gracias," I say.

The circle of kids mimic my voice, a mushy echo of their hard-edged words.

Orange curtains cover Luz's windows, and Mexican and American flags flank her door. I've always loved the Mexican flag, Christmas with an eagle and snake in between. On Luz's steps, cacti rise in spiny shapes from blue and purple pots. The curtains dance in one window, and she whips open the door.

"Pero, ¿qué carajo? Ginny, what are you doing here?"

Luz is wearing tight jeans and a scrunchy red-and-white top. I never realized how pretty she was, since she seems to pull on misery with her Run-Rite Inn shirt. Luz looks from side to side and waves for me to come in. The quick movements of her eyes tell me a hundred people already know a fat gringa has come to visit her.

Luz's trailer is a rich world of browns, oranges, reds, and golds. From what she's told me, she and her boys live with an older woman who needs her help; Pili and Mari share with two other women nearby. A worried voice calls from a distant room, and Luz answers reassuringly. She stands proud and important in her kitchen with its wooden cabinets and steel sink.

"New look?" Luz nudges me with amusement, gazing down at my green toes. "You come down here to show it off? Come in the living room. I'll make you a coffee."

Crystals of Nescafé spill on the green counter as she spoons them into white cups.

Luz's trailer has rooms so distinct you'd swear you were in a thick-walled house. Beyond the kitchen lies a warm space lined with wooden panels. A plaid couch softens one corner and extends along two walls. A flat-screen TV covers most of the wall opposite the couch. A wooden coffee table holds magazines from which tall, full-lipped women stare. Over the couch, on either side of the window, hang pictures of white houses under blue skies.

With their backs to the table, Rafa and a smaller boy are pushing buttons on bat-shaped remotes. With their fingers, they're guiding warriors in brown skirts who are hacking each other with swords. They cry out with delight at the sounds of the game: airy swoops when they miss, jagged gasps when they hit. There are even cool clangs when their swords clash in midair.

"¡Rafa, baja eso!" orders Luz as she sets our cups on a magazine face.

Rafa scowls and jabs a button, and the fight to the death dims.

"That's amazing," I say. Together, the slim dark TV and the marvelous game must be worth a thousand dollars.

Luz looks down at her boys, and for a moment her eyes warm. In the lamplight, their hair is more chestnut than black. Rafa winces at a blow from his younger brother's warrior.

"So this is Rafa and …"

"Manuel," she says quickly.

I reach for a white mug of coffee to save the model's burning face. She has wide brown eyes like Luz's, rimmed with curves of elegant black. Except for the day without power, I have never seen Luz without makeup, and even that morning, she looked strong. My eyes look like two marbles that somebody shoved into a melting snowman.

Luz spreads her fingers on her cup to warm them and breathes slowly as she looks me up and down. Manuel gasps at a swipe that nearly lops off his fighter's head.

"Their father sent money," says Luz. "He got a job. I went to Jones City, and I bought this. Now nobody's chasing the wind. They stay in here all day long."

Her dark eyes meet mine in a challenge.

"That's great," I say.

I wonder about the kids outside and shift my eyes toward the window. Luz reads my thoughts.

"We must have had fifty kids in here the first day," she says. "We had to make rules—how many at a time, when Rafa and Mani could play alone. Now everybody's gotten used to it. They've gone back to their old games."

My eyes drift to the screen, where Mani's warrior has skewered the other's thigh.

"¡Mierda!" gasps Rafa, and Luz yelps at him as his little brother grins.

The little one has a winning smile, but I prefer the one who chases clouds.

"Ginny." Luz catches me off balance. "Why did you come down here?"

I turn, and her dark eyes won't be denied.

"I'm thinking … thinking of working full time at the Haverford. Carl asked me. Not for breakfast—as a housekeeper."

"That's great!"

Luz smiles, and I sense many levels of gladness. She's wondering why I didn't tell her this at work.

"I'm just … not sure," I stumble. "Jake needs me. I don't want to hurt Jake."

Luz squinches up her face and blows air from her mouth as though she were smoking a cigarette.

"Jake does what's best for Jake. You should do what's best for you."

A white ruffle on her blouse trembles.

"Have you ever applied …"

Luz's face hardens, and a drop of coffee sears the model's face.

"Carl doesn't like Mexicans," she says. "He thinks we can't speak English. When he hires one, he makes sure she can't talk, so she can never prove him wrong."

I nod slowly and watch the warriors bend and whirl. Luz speaks to the boys in a river of Spanish. I realize I must be delaying their dinner.

"Thanks for the coffee," I say.

"You'll make more at the Haverford," says Luz. "You should go."

A hundred eyes follow me out even though the dark is erasing me.

15

Night comes differently to Balboa Street than it does to the glowing strip. No streetlights blink on when the edges of things blur into the darkness around them. Not that there's much to illuminate—no wooden houses this far down. I strain to make out the Bible church, a prefab structure with a steeple on top. It wouldn't make sense to light these streets, since everyone passing this way has headlights—except for the people who've been knocked loose. A soft rush of sound floats from the strip, but I might as well be on the open plains. Only the crunches of my feet tell me that I'm still on the road. I avoid this part of town at night because anything could be out there in the dark.

Now and then I pause to hear the sounds lurking below my grinding beat. Something tiny rustles in the grass pushing into the street's crumbling sides. The wind is fading, but enough force remains to trouble the sage. The night is drawing uneasy breaths. A pop pierces the blackness, and I jump—the backfire of a truck, or a distant shot. If I pass too close to a house, someone might aim a gun at me. I speed up my crunching rhythm, but that just means I hear less.

I stop to listen to the night breathe and stand immersed in a sea of sound. Each sage bush whispers a different curse to the air ruffling its leaves. Far off on the interstate, a motorcycle is grinding its way into the black. Otherwise, the sighs of traffic flow into the night like a river into an ocean. A faint crackle beside my feet betrays a small animal creeping by. Maybe a mouse, scared of coyotes but too hungry to stay in his hole. I wrap my arms around myself and strain to see the church's gleaming side. Only blackness meets my eyes, blackness alive and twisting with sound.

Something glides overhead with a whoosh like the sword swipes in Rafa and Mani's game. The boys' father couldn't have paid for that. From what Luz says, he melted into the night like that bird who just passed overhead. Nothing for five years, and then a thousand bucks? How did he know where to find her? Life might go better if all dads did that instead of sticking around to curse and hit. Just disappear and send in the bucks. Whoever paid for that game mustn't find out where Lành has gone. If she can't stay at the nail parlor or the trailer park, then she's going to have to stay with me. I just can't imagine how to get her from Manny's Body Shop to Houston.

An odd sound rises from the dirt on my left, a sound that no wind could make. Something is gulping the air and expelling it in groans. I freeze, but my left foot scans the ground for a rock. My heel hits a stone, and I grab it. The gulping and sobbing continue, and I realize these aren't the sounds of something that wants to hurt. I clutch the rock, its ridges biting my fingers.

"Hey," I call.

"Down here," grunts a voice.

A man is crushing the grass as he rolls, and I turn toward the sound.

"Jerry?"

Cloth rustles as he pushes himself upright.

"What are you doing out here?"

"I don't know." His gasp could be a laugh or a sob.

"Have you been ... out here ... since you left the Haverford?"

"Yeah. Out here. That's one way to put it."

Two brilliant eyes appear down the road, and I drop beside Jerry and push him down. My rock hits the soft dirt with a thud. People by the roadside make good targets because they're not likely to be missed. I lie with my arm pressing Jerry's back until the car crunches over a hump into the trailer park. The stink of Jerry says he's been on the streets, although what he's saying makes no sense. I slip my hand over what feels like his suit and settle far enough from him that I won't retch.

"Why don't you call your family?" I ask. "Or a friend? You're sick. It's okay to call."

Jerry breathes as though each lungful of air hurts.

"My wife left me a while back, before ... this. She took the girls. It's better they don't hear from me. There's no one else to call."

"Your job—your boss ..."

"Not anymore," he says.

With a grind and a flash, a car emerges from the trailer park, and Jerry drops without being told. His oily stench makes my stomach heave. The car's headlights catch the side of the Bible church a few hundred yards ahead.

"Have you been going to the church?" I ask. "Were you waiting for them to open?"

The Bible church holds services each night, and they never reject anyone. I've heard that Christians in the wooden houses take in drifters to clean up so that they can look for work.

"I haven't gone to the church," he says. "I have no right."

"*What did you do?*"

My voice tears into the night. Jerry's way of putting things makes me angry, saying no to everything in life.

"You can tell me," I say. "You did something, and you need to tell. I'm nobody. If you tell me, it won't matter."

Whisking sounds fill the darkness. Jerry must be brushing himself off.

"I was driving west," he says. "I was doing well. Clean for more than three months. I was getting used to it—Susan and the girls gone. I was going to look for a job in LA, and I actually thought I might find one. I just needed … And then I saw this ad."

"For a girl." My voice tumbles loose.

"Yeah. A hundred dollars. Innocent. Exotic."

I rub my arms, first one and then the other.

"Who got the hundred dollars?"

"Who knows?" Jerry shudders. "I typed in my credit card number—that was all. The girl was everything the ad said. But she couldn't talk to me—she was too scared. And I did it anyway. I felt her seize up from the pain—and I still did it." His voice breaks up into heaves.

"That's it? You didn't hit her?"

I can't believe he'd end up out here for having sex, no matter who with, no matter how scared.

"No!"

Jerry's horror speaks of a different kind of badness than the ones I know. From the way he's crashed, I thought we were going to find the next missing girl in the sage.

"Jerry," I say. The word tastes odd in my mouth. I never call anyone by name. "Why don't you call the police?"

"Are you kidding?" he says. "They'd kill me. Whoever's moving those girls—they'd find me and cut off my head."

"Cancel your credit card," I say. "Change your name. What happened to her—you could keep it from happening to other girls. You can't be worse off than you are now."

A car door clunks, and a woman's voice spills into the night. A crunch of tires answers her. It must be time for the Bible church service.

"Why haven't you called the police?" asks Jerry. "You seem to know plenty."

"Not yet."

I push myself up. The porch lights of the Bible church have changed the night to a dark universe that swirls around them. Even at that distance, they are strong enough to whiten my arm as I reach down to Jerry.

"I can show you the way out of here," I say. "Back up to the motels."

"I think I'll try the church," says Jerry. "I've been through this before."

16

It's hard to wash dishes with your stomach full. Once you've eaten, you don't want to know about food. But there it is, swirls of mustard on plates, reminding you of what you've stuffed into you. Mom and I used to wash up together, but once we moved in with Harper, I washed alone. Harper's trailer looked a lot like Luz's, except that I could see him and Mom on the couch, and they could watch me scrub. I tried not to clink the plates so as not to draw their eyes.

One night we had eaten macaroni and cheese, which had left the blue-and-white plates coated with orange glue. I loved those plates with the wavy blue spiderweb linking the pointed blue flowers. I wanted to save them from the orange goo that was covering their pattern like mold. That same orange was swelling my stomach, turning it to a heavy stone. No matter how much soap I used, the cheese still matted the sponge. The poor yellow thing only spread the cheese, like a dog that had rolled in orange mud.

Mom looked up from *Entertainment Tonight* while Harper's eyes stayed on the screen. She had slung her bare leg over his so that her pink toes rose like hills in his view. A force in her eyes scanned me as though she wished she could rub me out. She wanted to blink off my dad like a nightmare, but anytime she woke up, there I was. Mom's eyes had as many voices as colors, and another one told me she thought I looked sweet with my arms lost in her green gloves. Harper followed Mom's eyes to me and glared, warning me to hurry up.

The sink monster had long been quiet in his black can down below. All monsters seemed to live in cans, even the friendly ones on *Sesame Street*. I wondered if the sticky cheese would clog him, and I pushed clumps of it between the black petals guarding his hole. I finished the plates and wished I had done the glasses first because the sponge left greasy smears. When I saw the cheese pan full of bloated paste, my stomach clenched. Mom had poured in an inch of water, which had swollen a few lost noodles but done little else. Loose films of cheese shuddered while a brown crust clung fiercely to the steel wall. I poured the loose paste down the sink monster's throat and rubbed lemon soap into the sticky sponge. I gave a firm swipe, and the greasy pan shot out of my hand and banged the steel sink.

"Hey! What the fuck?"

Harper jumped to his feet.

"Can't we have any peace and quiet in here?"

Mom stayed stiff where she landed. I grabbed the pan to stop the clanging. Harper's steps made the blue-and-white plates shudder in their rack. His open hands trembled, looking for something to grab. He seized a plate and ran his middle finger across it.

"You call this clean? Hasn't anybody ever told you, when you do something, you need to do it right?"

With a clatter, he stacked the plates in the sink and flooded them with water. He picked up the cheese-infested sponge, then threw it down in disgust. I don't think that Harper had washed many dishes.

"Looks like you need something stronger," he muttered. "Something that'll cut through that grease."

Under the sink, he shoved bottles into each other until he found what he wanted.

"Oh, yeah." He grinned. "This stuff sinks in real good."

He was holding a yellow can of oven cleaner.

"Are you crazy? That stuff is deadly!" Mom stood in the kitchen door, aghast.

The sharp-scented foam could turn black oven crust to jelly in less than a minute. Harper whirled around and pointed the red nozzle at her, laughing. She screamed and whipped her arm across her eyes. Harper stared at the red hole, wishing for a target.

"Didn't I tell you not to disturb us in there?" he asked.

"I'm sorry," I murmured. "The pan—"

"Did I tell you, yes or no?"

I held my breath.

"I guess it didn't sink in," said Harper.

He grabbed my arm, shoved the green glove down, and sprayed a foamy worm onto my skin. Mom screamed and rushed forward, but Harper blocked the sink.

"Nobody touches that faucet until she learns to listen."

The white worm crackled as he settled, burning his way in. I couldn't move. Mom tried to drag me toward the bathroom, but Harper now guarded the kitchen door. The searing white worm was stealing my breath. The kitchen was turning to gray snow.

"Harper, please!" begged my mother.

Harper was laughing and she was crying as she blasted

my arm with water. The green glove I was still wearing filled with burning suds.

When Mom turned off the water, the worm had left a long red streak on my arm. I wondered how a white worm could leave red tracks, but with time, the red trail turned as white as the worm that had blazed it. Red turned into white every time, as though the worm wanted me to remember what he looked like.

17

Although I'm worried about Jerry, I have never felt more relieved to walk along the strip's gritty concrete. Manny has turned off his sign, but a crack of light over his garage door betrays the gathering inside. I hover in the glow, uncertain how to knock. A side door whips open, and Manny appears, gripping a tire iron. Behind him stands the curly-haired boy, holding a pistol and looking more scared than ever.

"Ginny!" laughs Manny. "Everything all right?"

I shake my head, and he waves for the boy to go inside. Manny glances up and down the sidewalk, then unlocks his office. He offers me his green swivel chair and scrapes a metal one across the floor for himself.

"You don't look good. What's going on?" he asks.

Manny's thick brown hair shines he's got it pulled so tight. Only a few escaped strands drift around his forehead, seeking a better place to lie. The bright desk lamp reveals that his aging snake tattoos have blurred. His dark eyes look anxiously into mine, trying to read the deadly thing I have to say.

"I found a girl in a dumpster. A Vietnamese girl."

"Shit." Manny's arms tighten in a way that says this is worse than what he thought he'd hear. He swallows and brings his eyes back to mine. "Alive?"

I breathe in and out but can't speak.

"You found her today? At the Run-Rite Inn? Where is she right now?"

His whole office is staring: steel shelves full of papers about wounded cars.

"She's at the nail parlor," I murmur. "But they won't keep her."

Manny nods as if to say that's the first place he'd try too.

"So why is this your problem?" His voice is a soft growl.

"I don't know." The metal legs of his chair stand tense. "I found her. People want to hurt her. She was just there . . . so scared. I can't let them hurt her."

Manny draws a deep breath, and the light shines on his slick hair. "You don't want to bring her here, do you?"

"Yeah. I was going to ask Luz—down at the trailer park—but I couldn't."

"Does Luz know about this?" Manny straightens. "Who knows besides you?"

A truck roars outside, then clears its throat to let out a higher-pitched cry.

"Just Heather at Never-Ending Nails—the old lady. She knows a place in Houston where the girl can go. But someone has to drive her."

I pull the tightly folded paper from my pocket.

"Why couldn't you ask Luz?"

Manny hasn't moved. For the first time since I found the girl, my insides start to heave.

"Because … because … I think she got money …"

"Shit!" Manny slams his fist into his thigh. He leans forward to grip my shoulders.

"You know what you're doing? Who you're dealing with?

They're going to come after this girl. They'll kill anyone who gets in their way."

His chair's silver legs stand burning clean in the electric light.

"I had to help her," I say.

"Yeah, I know the feeling."

Manny gathers me into his snake arms. He smells of oil and beer and sweat. My cheek is crushed against his chest. His heart is thumping in my ear.

"Okay." He releases me and looks me up and down. "If we're going to do this, we have to move fast. Jimmy can drive you." Manny laughs at my frown. "Yeah, big man with the gun. You're safer with him than anyone."

"But I'm not going," I say, confused.

"The fuck you're not," says Manny. His eyes brighten to the color of coffee. "You're alive now, and I want you to stay that way."

"No." I scowl at my alien-green toes.

"Look, you seem pretty smart," says Manny. "What do you think they're going to do? A bunch of guys are probably on their way here right now. They'll talk to Luz, that big manager guy—" Manny breaks off as he reads my face. "Oh, fuck. That's it, isn't it?"

My skin has caught fire.

"You want to protect that guy? That fat manager?"

Tears slide out, and the heaves keep coming.

"What did he ever do for you?" asks Manny. "Besides give you a job cleaning rooms."

"He … treats me like a person! Like you! I would do the same thing for you!"

"Sh!" orders Manny, and I realize I must have shouted.

"He's got to be in on this," he says quietly. "If someone's moving girls and they're staying at the Run-Rite Inn, the manager's got to know. You're risking your life to save a girl and risking it again to save the guy who's hurting her? He may treat you like a person, but he's using those girls worse than animals."

Manny's eyes are peeling me, and I'm falling away in layers.

"What can you do, anyway?" he demands.

"I ... I just need to be there," I say.

"You think this guy cares for you?" asks Manny. "I thought you ... Let me ask you something. If you could sleep tonight with anyone you wanted—not sex, just sleep— just lie there with your arms around someone, who would it be?"

"Judy," I whisper. "The girl at Never-Ending Nails."

Manny's eyes glisten, and he looks toward his bookcase.

"That's what I thought," he murmurs. "You've got to be careful."

He turns back to me and takes my hands. "They kill people like us," he says. "They tried to kill Jimmy. You'd be better off in Houston. You might find a woman like you."

With my eyes fixed on Manny's, I shake my head.

"If I go, won't they come after you?" I ask. "They'll know I found her, and who else would drive us there? If I stay, they'll think I don't know anything. That's better for you and Jake."

Manny leans back in his chair and rubs his swollen eyes.

"You are smart," he says. "Jake. So that's his name. I hope he's worth getting your head busted."

"I'm not afraid," I say.

18

Harper liked to work, so he didn't spend much time at home. He woke up at five and made sure we got up with him so we could eat breakfast together.

"That's the difference between a working man and a bum," he said. "The ability to get out of bed."

Mom would fry him eggs, which he liked to mash between two pieces of toast. As she nudged the eggs around the pan, her silky blue robe quivered, and he watched her with satisfaction. By six Harper was gone to lay glossy seas of wooden floor. When he came home at night, he would tell us about floors like golden meadows, like chocolate lakes. And all the people who walked on them were fools. Not one of them deserved that much space. People who couldn't drive a nail themselves thought they were better than the guys who built their homes.

Still, Harper was proud of his work, the way he was proud of Mom. He called her the prettiest woman in the state, and she took pains to make him think so. He telephoned her to make sure she had reached work at Sarah's Salon and then again at lunch to ask what she had planned for dinner. In the few hours he had at home at night, he wanted everything perfect.

I stayed in the kitchen doing my homework, trying to

make sense of the numbers split by slashes. Under my math book, the sprigged white tabletop rested on four silver legs. The chrome chairs with white cushions matched the table, but I didn't like them at all. When the cold metal touched my legs, I slid them aside.

One day I came home from school feeling as though I'd been packed in cotton. When Mom got home, she said I looked flushed and held her cool hand against my forehead.

"Oh, yeah," she murmured. "We'd better get you to bed."

Mom didn't have a thermometer, but when I coughed soup into the toilet, she said I had the flu. She brought me a bucket and a bag of frozen peas to lay across my forehead. The way she said "flu," I sensed she was afraid of something worse than my being sick.

The next morning, Harper woke up burning, even though Mom felt fine. For the first time in his life, Harper called in sick and lay fuming under a yellow blanket. Mom had to go to work, but between customers, she kept calling him. I lay on one side of the wall Harper had built, splitting the bedroom. He lay on the other, talking to Mom.

"Fucking Typhoid Mary," he muttered. "Never been sick a day in my life."

By midday I was starting to feel stronger and crept out of bed to look for food. I eased the refrigerator door open, but the bottles shivered. Harper coughed and rolled. His feet hit the floor with a thud. I counted his steps across the living room. One. Two. Three. His body filled the doorway, blue-striped pajamas and red-brown hair. His golden-brown eyes glowed strangely.

"Guess not even the flu can take away your appetite."

I stood frozen, clutching the refrigerator door.

"Close that thing. Stop wasting energy."

I shut the door fast, and the bottles shivered. Harper straightened his twisted pajamas and considered what to do with me.

"I don't like you sneaking around," he said. "You can fool your mom but not me. You're a little sneak."

He strode heavily back to the bedroom, and I pulled the door open. The seal stuck, and the bottles clinked when it gave. Harper was smiling when he returned with three bathrobe belts dangling from his hand. His dark blue terry cloth and Mom's pale blue silk hung like entwined snakes. The thicker brown one I didn't recognize.

"Sit down in that chair," he ordered. "I'm going to stop you sneaking around for one goddamn day."

He lashed each of my legs to the metal chair so tight its cold invaded me. With the brown belt he bound my arms together while he breathed heavily in my face. I felt the relief in his hands, which were working for the first time all day. Harper stepped back and regarded me.

"That should take care of you. No more creeping around. I don't want to hear a sound from you. Your mom should have done this long ago."

He walked determinedly back to the bedroom, and when I heard his far-off snores, I breathed deeper. Winter light was brightening the white table, but it couldn't warm those chair legs. My eyes traveled around the room, asking the walls for help. The refrigerator sang on and off, and the wooden cabinets stayed shut. The whole room seemed annoyed with me, an intruder caught in its space.

As the light faded, I got hungry, but I didn't dare scrape the chair across the floor. I couldn't feel my hands or feet, and I wasn't sure they still worked. The real problem was I had to go to the bathroom. I had stopped coughing up food, and it wanted to come out. Fat bubbles of stink passed through me, telling me to get to a bathroom fast. I pictured a giant brown worm pushing his way out and tried to suck him back in. I tried so hard I stopped breathing, and the kitchen turned to gray mush. The worm won. In the end I even helped. I pushed, and he slithered out into a hollow under my bottom. The room filled with a stink so bad the walls tried to pull away from me.

Grayness had taken over the room when Harper appeared in the door. He flicked on the light, and I closed my eyes just after I saw his flushed face.

"What's that—" He cut off abruptly. "Oh, Jesus, you nasty, filthy little shit!"

He raised his hand to smack me but stopped as though he were afraid to get it dirty.

"Don't look at me like that!" he roared.

My swollen feet were purple under the coils of blue belt.

"I've got to throw her out of here," he muttered. "I can't take this. Know how many hot women are out there with no fucking freaks attached?"

Harper's fingers worked the air as though he wished it were made of wood. He turned and took one step toward the bedroom, then suddenly changed his mind. He whirled and brought the heel of his hand smashing up into my face. He didn't hesitate, as though he had been practicing this move a thousand times in his head. I watched the hard cup of his hand coming slowly to meet my nose. The chair tilted back an inch at a time. It clattered dully when it hit the floor, muffled by a hard, wet sound.

19

I come to the Run-Rite Inn at nine the next morning, just the way that Heather said. My set face keeps wanting to creep into new positions. I can't remember how my eyes and mouth used to feel on a normal day. I could take lessons from Jake, who greets me like a man who's been dreaming through the night. His thick arms move through the air as though he's swimming. The curves of his shoulders speak of a weight no greater than clearing the rooms for checkout. What if Manny is wrong, and one of the night managers is selling the girls? Frank would do it gladly, but he doesn't seem smart enough. Jake's blue-green eyes are fixed on me.

"Did Carl give you some time to decide?" His voice, like his body, flows smoothly.

"Yeah. A week." I nod.

"I'd hate to lose you," he says. "But it's a great opportunity."

Luz pushes through the office door, her arms tense as though her boys are sick. She looks from me to Jake and scowls.

"You two thinking up a way for the rooms to clean themselves?"

"Ease up," says Jake. "Ginny's just talking to me for a second."

Luz yanks the door as though it were heavier than it is. Her voice hisses in the breezeway. "Blanquitos de mierda."

Once Luz gives me my quarter, she avoids me, and she keeps Marielena close. She puts me in rooms I rarely clean, the ground-level strip facing Frontage Road. Construction workers like these rooms best, since they can park their trucks outside their doors. They don't have to worry about break-ins the way women do. After a day of hoisting tiles or driving toward their next job, they're too tired to trash their rooms. The worst they can offer me is smooth brown cakes of dirt that crumble to dust in my hands.

I keep watch for the men that Manny and Heather dread, but no one appears, unless he's well disguised. My rooms house dark-skinned men in work boots and gray-haired gringo tourists who stare at the coffee, trying to conjure a breakfast. Maybe the loss of one girl isn't as big a deal as Manny claims. Maybe they'll think she ran off into the sage and owes her freedom to no one but herself.

At the Haverford, I handle the rooms of late checkouts, fussy people who like to sleep and watch TV. They don't muss their rooms, but they unfold each towel. They inspect each object with their fingers, as though they have to knead them all to get their $119 worth.

As the light fades, the strip holds its breath on this clear day without wind. I scan each blank storefront for Jerry, but he's gone. I glance through the glass front of Never-Ending Nails, but Heather glares and waves me on. Judy is hunched over a woman's feet, her slim back tense under her blue shirt.

When the darkness comes, I slip into my room, feeling more alone than I ever have. A soft knock rattles the door, and my heart explodes to life.

"Who's there?" I call across the bolts.

"It's Manny," answers a soft voice.

I slide the chains, and Manny's eyes circle my room, sadly greeting the scrubbed furniture.

"Jimmy made it to Houston," he says. "He found Heather's cousin. Your girl should be safe there for a while. He says it's just a regular nail parlor."

My heart hasn't slowed, and I stand with my fingers frozen to the last lock. Manny keeps his black eyes on mine.

"You know, Jimmy's going to stay down there. You should go too. You haven't seen anything—anyone?"

"No." I shake my head.

"Just because you haven't seen them doesn't mean they aren't here," says Manny. "It's the ones you don't see you have to worry about."

His voice fills the room, so that even when he's gone, his words turn in slow circles around the ceiling. *Forensic Team* soothes me into an uneasy sleep.

I wake with a jolt as though someone hit me, but I'm lying alone in liquid black. I thought I heard a cry like a kitten's mew, but the windless night is still. I sit up in bed and taste the darkness with my ears. Only my breathing stirs the air, a faint flow in and out. Something is wrong in the night, but the wrongness isn't in this room. The blue numbers on the clock say 2:02. Jake will be home in bed in Pinto, maybe with that sensational girl. Anything he's allowing to happen is going to be happening right now. I push myself up, and the cold air grasps me. I pull on a gray hoodie and dark pants.

I've never been on the strip at two in the morning, and its persistent life surprises me. I tuck in my hair and plod along so that I'll look like a homeless man seeking shelter. About every thirty seconds, a car swishes softly down the Merrill Highway. Anytime lights approach, I turn aside so that they can't see my pale woman's face. Who knows what these men are seeking as they glide past the dark strips sealed against the night? Maybe they're sick of pools of light on I-50, and their eyes are hungry for solid shapes. I sense them gazing at me as a small human shadow on the move. I try to take long steps like a man, since at two in the morning, even a fat woman with a smashed face is better than none at all.

In the Roundabout lot, two men are laughing as they share a beer. They beckon me, but I hunch my shoulders and burn my way up the hill. The blue Run-Rite Inn sign is branding itself into the night. I approach softly—toe first, then heel—so that my feet don't crunch in the grit. Stuart's profile in the brightly lit office tells me I have little to fear. Stuart is our most timid night manager, a skinny kid who studies through his shift. He sees the job as twelve free hours of computer time and hates to leave the office's warm lights. His black hair lies limply on his head, and his dark-rimmed glasses flash as he smiles at something online. He has formed a mind meld with Jake's computer that only a blackout could break.

I creep toward the stairway farthest from the office and pause to listen on each step. Trucks moan on I-50, and cars sigh as they rise toward the open interstate. What an awful fortress this motel makes, designed to be entered on each side. I slip along the walkway toward the back rooms, the 200s facing the slope and highway. Nothing that happens there can be heard unless someone is listening. I glide from door to door like a ghost hungry for sound. From 228 I hear snores; from 222, a burst of machine-made laughter. I freeze at the dull clang of a foot on the stairs. Someone else is moving about. I flatten myself against the wall, but the bright lights have me. There is nowhere to disappear. The clangs sound heavy and regular, but they're fading. I wait until they've died away, then press my ear to 220.

I jump as I hear the mew from my dream, which is now almost a shriek.

"¡No! ¡Por favor!"

Marielena!

The door of 220 has never worked well, and I kick it as hard as I can. It cries out once, bewildered, and then gives with the second blow.

Marielena is squirming on the bed. Her wrists and ankles are tied with white rope. She is wearing her blue sequin dress, but its skirt has been forced up to her waist. Black strands of hair are stuck to her face, which is wet with tears. A fat, red-haired man turns from her to me, his jaw slack with astonishment. Before he can move, I grab the lamp. Its cord snaps. I swing the pottery base in an arc that ends with his head. The lamp breaks with a wet crunch, and he falls onto the bed. Marielena screams and twists and rolls to the floor with a thud. Once the bristly man is lying, I hit him again and again. I pound his head as though it's a bump that I have to flatten out. The lamp has split into jagged pieces, but I smash him with the ones in my grip.

Another voice has joined Marielena's, a deeper, booming bass. In the doorway stands a fat woman with gray curls. She is pointing a short-nosed gun.

"FBI!" she shouts. "Don't move. Stop hitting that man."

20

So that was why she was hovering. Not to sell chubby figurines in gift shops. The sturdy grandmother makes the unlikeliest agent ever, but why not? Anyone who caught her prowling at two in the morning would think she was after a Snickers bar to increase the pleasure of her sexy book. She introduces herself—Carla Bauer is her name—and says we need to ride to Jones City. The man with the bloody head is going to the hospital; me and Marielena, to the police station. Arrow's strip mall police office can't handle exportations or FBI interrogations, which we are about to face.

The redheaded man heaves and moans. He is shoveled into an ambulance, but Mari and I ride in a squad car. Red and blue lights blaze outside Never-Ending Nails, and I twist my neck to see. A black, smoking hollow has opened in the familiar strip. I squeeze Mari's hand.

"Everything is going to be all right," I say. I strain to recall a sound. "Bien."

Mari looks at me with the faintest smile, grateful to me for lying.

By five Carla has me behind a metal table that holds two paper cups of coffee. The interview room is a scratched cell half the size of my room at Manny's. Dark scrapes mar every wall, left by bodies angry at being stuffed into this space. Carla's curls lie askew, and her face droops, but she sits as though she couldn't care less. She rests her elbows on the table with a patience that scares me worse than an attack. She wants to clean me out, and she isn't in a rush. She studies my face a long time before she speaks.

"How old were you—when that happened?" she asks.

I run my fingers over my nose and lips.

"Somebody hit you—but they didn't fix it. They could have, but they didn't."

"Insurance didn't cover it." My voice spills out. "They said I needed plastic surgery. I was ten."

In her pale blue T-shirt, Carla looks like the ladies who sell me cookies at Dollar World. She folds her soft arms.

"Where is he now? The guy who did that?"

"I don't know," I say.

The policewoman never let me go home from the hospital. She sent me into foster care. Mom made a fuss, but her eyes weren't angry. When I looked into them, the blue particles swam apart. Now she could give Harper the family he wanted, his own children, a clean start.

"Looks like you learned to hit pretty good," says Carla. "It's lucky that guy had a hard head. He's going to make it. You're up on assault but not on murder charges."

I shrug my shoulders. Nothing in my life ever felt better than smashing that bristly pig's head.

Carla narrows her eyes. "This is serious, you know. You could go to jail."

"He was hurting Marielena," I say.

My voice speaks without me bothering to shape it. I

wonder if this is how other people talk, the ones who find words so easily.

"Marielena's your friend?" asks Carla.

I shift my feet and meet the chill legs of the metal table.

"Is she your girlfriend?" she presses.

"No!" I gasp. "We work together. I show her things."

"Like how to make money with guys on the net?"

"No!" I jump to my feet.

"Sit down," commands Carla. "So who did teach her? We can help you if you help us."

"Could you help Marielena?" I blurt.

Carla nods slowly, her face blank. "I could talk with immigration. See what I can do."

"Girls are staying at our motel," I murmur. "Vietnamese girls—on their way to somewhere. And when they stay overnight …"

Carla's heavy features lie still. I'm not telling her anything she doesn't know.

"It would take a manager to run that," she says. "Which one's doing it?"

A brown smear on the wall forms an arc over her head.

"Yeah, it takes a village," she mutters. "And that nail parlor that burned a few hours ago—you don't know anything about that either?"

Carla dissolves into a gray blur.

"Heather, Judy—are they all right?"

"No one was in there," she says. "No one got hurt. You know where those women went?"

I blink to clear my sight. "No."

Carla takes a deep breath and straightens. "I'm going to ask you again," she says. "One of your managers is pimping

113

underage girls. Little girls—foreign girls—like your friend you were trying to help. You almost killed some idiot who paid him a hundred bucks. Why protect the one who sold her?"

All Jake's looks at Marielena—he never wanted her for himself. A girl went missing, and he just replaced her, one girl for another. Luz would have gone along, even though she didn't want to. She'd sell anyone to keep Rafa and Mani safe. If she thought she was going to lose that money—or her job or her life—she'd give Jake anyone he wanted. Raising money for his online school—why couldn't he just do like Stuart? Take morning classes at the community college and pay for them by working nights. But then the Run-Rite Inn wouldn't be his motel.

Carla's eyes have more intensity than color. "I know what's happening," she says. "It didn't take me a day. You wouldn't be telling me anything I don't know. Just confirming it."

"One girl for another." I realize I'm talking out loud. "Like they were things."

"Is he doing anything for you?" asks Carla. "He couldn't do this without his top women knowing. Does he hand you a twenty here and there—just to keep quiet?"

"No!" I cry. "I wouldn't take that kind of money. That's why ... he's ... trying to get rid of me. It's Jake. He lost a girl, and he gave them Marielena."

21

Carla teaches me to disappear in ways I never knew I could. I leave straight from my talk with her, and I don't take a thing with me. I can't tell Manny where I'm going—too risky, Carla says. Whoever burned Never-Ending Nails will be looking for me. I offer to wait for them as bait, but Carla sets her lips in a hard line.

"We don't do that," she says.

She must have been tracking these people for months, and a pulse of blue in her eye says she's tempted. She might use Jake, Luz, or even Pili to set a trap. I don't know why, but she seems to like me in ways that only Jake and Manny ever have. Her officers seize Jake when he comes to work. They warn Manny, and I picture him sadly leaving his shop. I can move as easily as a rat, but how do you move a safe place that you've spent your whole life building?

As the FBI car rises onto I-50 East, I feel as though hands are heaving me upward. I've always been attached to the ground, and I love this throb in my guts as we flow onto the interstate. Only now do I realize how much I've wanted to spread my arms and glide with the wind. Like Rafa, I've always wanted to grab a ride and see where the air is going. I would love to follow it to the sea, to a place where the world opens out. I want to feel free to breathe, to watch the water washing the land.

We drive all the way to Houston, a hot, wet place with sticky gray streets and pale trees full of screaming birds. Carla stays more interested in me than she needs to be. I suspect she has picked my new home in a motel converted to brown apartments. I have windows here, high and wide, overlooking a battered street. Cars and trucks never stop rubbing its surface, which has split into open wounds. The traffic makes different music than it did in Arrow, a low, provoking growl. I have to buy blinds to cover the windows, or I could be seen by each passing car. They wouldn't see much but a squat woman scrubbing, but I want to keep my movements to myself. I scour the walls to take possession of the place, but the last renter has cleaned them well. I think she had a little girl because here and there I find loops of silver crayon, never higher than my chin.

I don't spend much time in my blank apartment, because my new life comes with a new job. Suddenly, I am cleaning rooms in a glass palace next to two monstrous hospitals. No construction workers stay here, or golosos or big families. The hushed place is a hive of sadness, housing people who can't eat or sleep. In every drawer, I check stiff brochures showing the wonders of this motel: a turquoise pool, salmon salad at any hour, lovely women who put smooth black stones on your back. These rooms don't speak to me the way the Run-Rite Inn rooms did, since they're too dignified to cry for help. They rarely need me because the stricken people who stay there barely touch them. Sometimes they kick their sheets to froth, but they never soil the gleaming showers. The trash they leave falls smoothly from the whispering liners. Their bodies and souls hover across the street, where the people they love are hurting.

Some of the deep wooden drawers have phone books, and I copy the address of each nail salon. My toes turn from green to pink to coral, but I can't find Heather, Judy, or Lành. I don't ask, but I speak with every woman who kneads my feet. The younger ones are studying to be accountants, physical therapists, and nurses. Most of them speak better English than Heather, some of them better than me. As they rub orange lotion into my calves, I picture a shining shop with green leaves drinking sun in the front window. Judy might become a nurse, and Lành, a therapist who teaches soldiers to walk on metal legs. Judy smiles at a dark-haired boy too proud to cry during his shot. They might work in any city but Wichita, that awful place the white van was going.

In the huge hotel, no one comes to watch me clean or feed me bits of news. When the vacuum doesn't roar, I can hear only the room's hushed breath. I think of the men who will come to Manny's and find only an echoing, greasy cave. I think of Marielena, headed for Mexico on a bus with strange men stroking her hair. Like the girl before her, she must have peeled that sparkly blue dress from her skin and hurled it in the trash.

Most of the time I think of Jake, who must be choosing between ways to be crushed. If he says who was driving the van to Wichita, he'll die, whether he's free, in prison, or hiding. If he doesn't tell, he'll get the maximum penalty for selling girls night by night. *I am helping to make that happen,* I think as tissues float from a golden can into my cart. A skinny lawyer has been coaching me in a slow, high-pitched voice. I have to testify about three in a room, the mystery van, and an illegal housekeeper sold to a red-haired man at night. The lawyer talks as though I don't understand what I saw, as if I were a bird learning to sing the words.

At the trial, the star witness isn't me but Jerry. I could have told the lawyer that. People listen to me even less than they look, and I like to keep it that way. If they ever saw me, they would start to think about everything they could get from me. Jerry looks as though he belongs in his gray suit, and his voice has lost its whining edge. He tells of the internet ad he saw and the call that led him to the Run-Rite Inn. The lawyers argue about cell phone towers and IP addresses, chasing each other like dogs around a central question: Did Jake make this happen?

Jake's lawyer swears that he knew nothing; the traffickers pimped the girls themselves. Like the lawyers, I know it will come down to looks. Would the heavyset, round-faced man in the blue suit sell a girl as if she were a thing? My eyes sting as I watch Jake meet their eyes, his thick arms resting on the table. He looks like the owner of a motel chain who respects each guest in its soothing rooms. Jake glances at me only once, a jolt so quick I can't tell whether he blames me for his ten-year sentence.

For months I clean the cold, sad rooms, and I feel nothing at all. I don't hear from Carla, and I suspect that she's lost the men driving the Vietnamese women. Jake won't talk, and no one else knows enough. Houston's broad streets gleam with cars that look as though they want to flatten me with their polished tires. The white sidewalks stick to my feet where splats of sweet drinks have landed. Seagulls cut curves in the sky, and a heavy softness tells me the sea is near. The buildings don't form sharp edges as they did in Arrow, where every wall seemed to slice the sky. Just once I'd like to see the Gulf, where the wet land, air, and water meet. New spirits could twist out of that murk, turning, unfolding in the gray.

From the high-voiced lawyer, I learn that Jake is in Beaufort State Prison, not far from Arrow. I trade the five-dollar bills the guests have left me for a round-trip Greyhound bus ticket. From the outside, Beaufort State frightens me worse than any place I've ever seen. Spirals of razor wire top dusty walls no one could climb even in his mind. I bounce toward the gate in a school bus of visitors and grit my teeth as strange hands squeeze my legs. A woman with a hard jaw inspects our clothes and orders a dark-haired girl to stay behind. She is wearing a red tank top that can barely hold her rounded breasts. She looks bewildered at first, but then her face crumples, and she raises her hands to her eyes. An older woman wraps her arms around her and stays back with her, though the gray-haired one is free to pass.

A frizzy-haired guard seats me at a window in the craziest room I have ever seen. It's a long, thin strip like a patch of ocean outside the portholes of a ship. The glass of my window is begging to be freed from the greasy smears defacing it. I wish that I had brought some green spray, but I'm not allowed to carry a thing, not even one paper dollar.

An imposter's face appears behind the thick glass reinforced with chicken wire. A hollow-cheeked man stares out at me, tense as a sprinter in his orange shirt. A purple cut extends from one eye, and his lower lip is swollen. Jake has lost weight and, with it, every trace of his managerial air. He looks as he might have the very first day that he applied for work at a motel. He recognizes me but freezes, as though trying to control an impulse. Maybe I'm the first person to visit him. Maybe that luscious girl Luz's friend saw with him hasn't come, maybe not even his mom.

Jake speaks softly, struggling. "Thank you for coming."

I open my mouth, but I can't speak. I have no idea why I'm here. Jake can't tell me anything that matters, since machines are recording every word. I raise my hand to the window, and Jake's rises to mirror it. Our fingers rest in the smears the people before us have left.

"I have a good job," I say. "In a beautiful motel."

"You can do more than clean," says Jake. "You're good for more than that."

His blue-green eyes look at me as though I were something good to eat. For a moment, I wonder whether if I were beautiful, he would have given me to the men instead of Mari.

"Everyone is good for a lot of things," I say. "You can't replace one person with another."

Jake keeps his eyes on me and nods solemnly. "You're right," he says. His lips twitch, and he leans forward. "Tell me about your motel."

And so, in the half hour we have together, I tell him about piles of white pillows, brown marble counters, and showers where you can turn with your arms spread wide and never touch the ceramic walls.

22

I start to walk all over Houston, feeling trapped inside its rushing rings. Such a strange, hot, wet place, with streets like the spokes of a wheel. I walk south one day until I hit the first ring in a world of pawn shops and package stores. On a concrete island, a woman in black leggings stands like a living statue. Across eight lanes of service road, I spot a blue sign. Beyond the elevated ring stands the biggest Run-Rite Inn that I have ever seen. On the third-floor balcony, traveling workers in blue caps watch me walking across the lot. In a row of bushy trees behind the motel, an unseen flock of birds scream. I stop, amazed, and a black bird emerges and shrieks as he shakes his jaunty tail. A white seagull glides down to perch on the roof of a black pickup truck. He turns his head with a jerk and scowls at me over his yellow beak. I must be hell to look at, but I have ceased to care. With a shudder, he raises his gray wings and flaps off toward the sea. If I stay here, I can follow him one day. The Gulf can't be far away. Gleaming glass warms my face. I have reached the office door. I watch the seagull until he dissolves into the gray, then push my way inside.

Acknowledgements

I am grateful to the many people whose support, guidance, and encouragement have helped me to write *Clean*. In the Warren Wilson MFA Program, I learned from my advisers Robert Boswell, Kirstin Valdez Quade, David Haynes, and Liam Callanan as *Clean* developed from a few scenes into a short novel. I am thankful to the Warren Wilson faculty and students who guided me in workshops, thesis preparation, and conversations: Director Debra Allbery, Charles Baxter, Kevin McIlvoy, Antonya Nelson, Sarah Stone, Kathy Crowley, Sarah Gauch, David Saltzman, Sonya Larson, and my kind, wonderfully supportive buddy Terri Leker.

The encouragement and teaching that have made me a better writer extend much further back in time. I owe my greatest debt to novelist Jim Grimsley, a colleague whose input has inspired and sustained me for the past fourteen years. I am also grateful to my colleagues Joseph Skibell and Lynna Williams. All three of these creative writers at Emory University took my writing seriously, offered guidance, and supported my decision to earn an MFA in fiction. I am thankful to my colleague at Hofstra University, Julia Markus, whose confidence and line editing twenty years ago helped convince me that my writing mattered. I am grateful to Diana Richmond, who inspired me at the 2008 Squaw Valley Writers' Workshop and introduced me to iUniverse. I appreciate the work of everyone at iUniverse who has helped to publish *Clean*, including Michelle Johnson, Joey Turvey, Donna Carlson, Nolan Estes, and my superb editor, Kelsey Adams.

I would like to thank Emory students Gabby Phan, Thalia Le, and Hung Nguyen and Warren Wilson students P. A. Le and Hieu Minh Nguyen, who offered me advice on Vietnamese language and culture. Any errors or misjudgments I have made in applying their ideas are my responsibility alone.

The line "Damn it, Janet," quoted on p. 10, is from *The Rocky Horror Picture Show*, screenplay by Richard O'Brien and Jim Sharman, © Twentieth Century Fox, 1975.

If I could spend additional years working on *Clean*, it might become a better book, but I no longer have those years to spend. The death of my beloved friend Antje Radeck at age fifty-five and the loss of my mother to dementia in her early sixties have convinced me that we need to give the world everything we can, while we can. So I offer *Clean* as it is today, alive, imperfect, and full of possibilities.

Printed in the United States
By Bookmasters